Donald Rich's Shaggy Dog

outskirts press

Outskirts Press, Inc.
http://www.outskirtspress.com

ISBN: 978-1-9772-2934-2

Outskirts Press and the "OP" logo are trademarks belonging to Outskirts Press, Inc.

PRINTED IN THE UNITED STATES OF AMERICA

Contents

The dictionary defines shaggy dog as a story of inconsequential happening that the teller finds humorous or interesting but to the reader or listener as boring and pointless.

Well, here you are. Judge for yourself.

Before you begin, however, let me thank Hannah Rich and Lexie Taylor, two of my granddaughters for all their help on this project, and of course their mothers, my daughters, for all their help with living every day.

The collection journey you are about to embark upon is the work of over 50 years.

We decided to divide the work into three sections.

1. The poetry and pearls section is pretty self-explanatory.

2. Not so much the family section. It is a group of essays about kids, the raising of kids and the fun we had doing it. There are also a couple about the most amazing lady I have ever known. The mother of the kids.

3. As for the prose section. Understand most of the entries were written to be read out loud. The punctuation (what there is of it) is poor and at times can be confusing.

You might want to try reading this section aloud yourself to get the most enjoyment.

You might wish to do this reading when you are in a room where no one can hear you and wonder what the heck you're talking about.

If you do read it in an area with other people able to hear you, please be prepared to be hauled off by a couple attendants, after they put you in an unflattering white jacket with sleeves that tie in the back.

If a condition of release is not getting the book back, you might consider small claims court. $19.95 plus shipping and handling.

Regardless, we hope you enjoy your reading before they drop the net.

Poetry and Pearls

I watched the little puppy
bring his new boy home
from the pet store.
They were both very excited.
So much so the little boy
wet his pants.
The puppy wasn't wearing any.

The diatribe emanating from her mouth settled on my soul like the image of a six dog back yard left unattended for a week.

When Parker County was voting on making their county a sanctuary city for the second amendment, every motion by the opposition was shot down.

Whether grilled, toasted or on fresh
white bread with mustard and mayonnaise;
Whether Munster, Swiss, Monterey jack,
Cheddar or even processed American.
It's not bad to eat, ask for, or be given a
cheese sandwich.
What is bad is someone else forcing the
choice for you.

To appreciate what you have received in the past, reflect on what you will give in the future.

When asked for an opinion on something that someone has just pontificated on, more than likely your response should be "get in line behind the scarecrow."

People always used to ask me for the Gettysburg address, but once we moved to Rhode Island, no one cared to ask me for the Pawtucket address.

Please remove me from your Christmas.
Thanksgiving, New Years, Hanukkah, Fourth
of July and Labor Day shopping lists. If you
plant a tree at your house, Arbor Day can remain.
I have transformed to an
asset-light lifestyle

Not mine, but important.
"Happiness is a condition of the mind…
Not a result of circumstances." -John Lubcock

Also not mine, but even more important.
"The two most important days of your life
are the day you are born and the day you
figure out why." -Mark Twain

Never put chapstick and a glue stick
in the same pocket.
Just saying.

The only time talent beats hard work is every time hard work takes a break.

The difference between jam and jelly is
you have never been caught in a
traffic jelly.

Tomorrow is going to come whether
you like it or not. Or not should
never be an option.

You do not have to see someone
to recognize their beauty.
Listen for a minute.

Also not mine.
"In a crisis the only asset you have is
Your credibility." -Paul Volker

Be careful what words you choose to use.
You can always offer an apology but you
can never take back the words.

Before you can boss, supervise, order,
cajole, manage or coach you have to teach.
More often than not, yourself as well,
Do not presume you know it all.

Criss cross is a game. It's a pattern in quilting and crossword puzzles. It is a song, it is a Hip Hop group and a ballad singer.
When you hear "Be all that you can be" that is what they are talking about.

Time transforms the hare into the
tortoise, but the determination and spirit
are doubled so don't bet against him for a
podium spot.

Life happens when you are busy
planning something else.

If you define yourself by other's perception of you, you will never be who you think you are.

The official rules of Chinese checkers say
the youngest person always starts the game.
So ask me again why I quit playing
about ten years ago.

Remember, a diamond is just a piece of coal that
experienced extreme pressure.
So if you are under pressure, just think
of yourself as a diamond in the making.

If you are the only Crayola in a box of number 2 pencils, do not worry. You will still be filling in with color when all else are dull or broken.

Your circle of friends is going to be quite small if they all have to be seismologists just to figure a way to get along.

Driving your bus trip of life, turn around
and look at the people riding with you.
If there is any person on that bus that you
would not trust driving, they need to be
off your bus.

The man was a wonderful human being but his band only had 73 trombones and 96 coronets.

If persons say "yes deere" they are
agriculturists. If they say "yes deer"
they are naturalists. If they say "yes dear"
they are romantics.
If they say, "during the next commercial"
They are in a long term relationship.

She has set the bar so high that for
the next person to succeed they will need
more than a Pole. I'm thinking also a
Czech and Ukrainian.

Here is a helpful hint. I sense you will
feel better if you spend some cents to
help improve the scents in your home.

Friendships and socks have a lot in common.
You can change them often if you like. The
difference. The socks you can get again from the dresser.
We do not have a drawer for friends.

Think about this and apply as necessary.
are you in love with the person,
or are you in love with the idea of being in love?

The light at the end of the tunnel gets
brighter as you get closer to it.
If you stand still or go backwards, it does
you absolutely no good.

Writing letters to old friends is like
going to a class reunion.
Except I can't be saying one thing
and thinking about how old they look.
If you want a letter from me,
send a picture.

If you have to pick –
far better a guitar than your nose.
You can't tune your nose.

I've never met a politician that didn't
tell me they would win.
I've yet to have one tell me I would.

It doesn't matter how you approach
riding a camel.
You still have to get over the humps.

An old Indian told me about walking
In another man's shoes,
And said it's philosophy.
The store clerk said it was
Shoplifting.

I sent you a rose
for your beauty.
I wrote you a poem
for your thoughts.
I gave you a wish
for your rapture.
And I'm sending you
Love for your Heart.

I couldn't find an angel for my Christmas tree
I found a Santa Claus,
Reindeer,
Drummer boys,
Gingerbread men and gingerbread houses,
But I couldn't find an Angel for my Christmas tree.

I found bells,
I found balls with glitter.
I found tinsel
and garlands made of gold.
But I couldn't find an Angel for my Christmas tree.

I looked in the department store,
the discount store,
the hardware store,
even the garden store.
But I couldn't find an Angel for my Christmas tree.

All I wanted was an angel for my Christmas tree.
The stores had garish foil,
Brass pillars,
Glass spirals with a nob on top.
But I could not find an Angel for my Christmas tree.

So, I went home
and with some cotton
and cloth
and buttons
and paint.
I made an Angel for my Christmas tree.

I put in love
I put in my heart's song of holiday joy,
and my thoughts of Christmas' meaning.
I had the Angel for my Christmas tree.

That is all that is on my tree this year.
My Angel.

Made for the most joyous season
and sending out to all who see her,
my best wishes for Christmas
and forever.

I couldn't buy an Angel for the Christmas tree
because her message had to come from me.

And it does.

The first contest, I knew I would win.
And I did.

My second contest I knew I'd win.
And I told everyone.
I lost.

My third contest I knew I'd win,
And I kept quiet.
People said I'd become humble.
I said I'd become experienced.
I won.

This morning I stood and watched
The clouds race through the mountain pass.
I guess they would have done that anyway.

A rainbow arched a frame of pastels
Around the greens and golds of nature's glory.
Nothing could stop that from being.

The mist of the early morning was
Dried by the bright sun that shone
Across the restless sea.

Every place I looked,
Everything I saw
Even the gentle old man,
His hands calloused by the strength he built,
His face weathered by the sorrow he endured.
His heart nurtured by the love he gave.
Another that you loved left today.
Finally, after so many clouds and mists,
so many rainbows and rising suns,
a brand new experience for him.
No tears. Just loneliness, good thoughts
wonderful memories, a smile and my turn to say,
"I'm proud of you."

If paper was the world, you would be the monarch.
If writing was the complete release, you would be free.
If thinking could make it so, it would have happened.
If acting was all that was necessary, everything would be
complete.
In a huge field of rock, one small flower defies nature's plan.
In a massive universe one person can change the world.
It all must happen together.

They stood for a moment and looked
into each other's eyes.
Seeing into, beyond and before.
Thousands of nights of loneliness.
Thousands of days of despair.
Looking back at each other,
sharing time that had been.
Without saying a word.
Sharing time that will still be there with the
Glow of a thousand tomorrows.
They stood and looked, embraced and dreamed.
Locked in the euphoria of togetherness.
Across the cloud-filled sky the sun shone through.
A ray of light.
A glimmer of hope.
A moment of rejoicing.
The day began again. The world started again.
And life was drops of time, consumed in love.

Aloha, little guy,
and welcome to the world.
David, is that the name?
or Dave,
or Davey.
Cherish that name.
It is one of the few things
you will ever be given in this life.
The rest you have to work for.
And to work with---
You have your own courage.
You have your own desire.
Today you are a cute little baby,
with bottles and rattles and toys.
Tomorrow you'll be a handsome boy,
with baseballs and footballs and school.

The next day a man with your part
of the world resting heavily on your shoulders.
Through it all
David,
Courage, desire and love.
It's a great start.
So, aloha little guy.
And welcome to the world.

If you were a goose, could you face the torturous
physical strain of annual migrations?
If you were a salmon, would you fight the currents
Of a cruel stream and the punishment of rocks on your body.
Killing yourself to spawn life for the same treatment?
If you were a rabbit,
would you daily run to the point of exhaustion
to escape those who would take your life?
If you were a squirrel, could you find energy to spend
every pleasant day finding food to tide you through the storm?
Would the industrious ant slave away each day if you were him?
Wouldn't always having to face the same to survive
Be more than a human could endure?
We have the prospect of a brighter tomorrow.

You know he will never forget all of the good times.
The bad times also weigh heavily upon his mind.
The neon sign that reads "dance tonight" is broken.
The old worn out building holds up a love-saddened old man.
More pathetic; the lock on the door, or the cold, bolted heart?
She is standing there now. Waiting to be swept away.
Oh, to waltz across the sea of happiness.
To dance on beaches of joy once more.
He goes back to rejoice
in the splendor of moments regained.
Times he so longs to be with her again.
No one can ever write their very last love song.

One lone light
shining across the city at night.
One lone tree
standing out on the mountain top.
A single tall building
casting its awesome shadow on the city skyline.
Built to stand alone,
Devised as a pinnacle of glory.
Whether it's by nature or by human creation,
Or by an infinite mold of only one.
There are some, even men, that can't help but be
Noticed and held in esteem, for they do stand out.
Nurtured by the good that they do.
Strengthened by the delight they deliver.
Motivated by their love and compelled by
The orbit of beauty.
Some stand as one strong, lone light.
The effort to be such a man is the height of being.

I watched a little boy hobble across the park
on crutches today.
Moving along the path as bicyclists weaved around him,
he stopped and watched a basketball game.
A mother chased her son in front of him and a
little girl almost knocked him down,
following an errant ball.
I watched a little boy hobble across the park
on crutches today.
Following a butterfly that could not be caught.
Stopping to pick a flower and clutching it in his
small hand against his wooden support.
I could see the gleam in the little boy's eyes
Today as I watched him make his way
Through a different world.
Doing those things he could,
Observing those things he couldn't do
but moving steadily through.
Oh, that we all had the courage, the drive, the strength
of the little boy on crutches—hobbling through the park today.

The world was a mural of clouds drifting past.
A shower of stars rained a rhythm of accompaniment
in the lonely nights vigil.
Minute squares of grain and grass.
Tiny valleys of rock.
Green trees dotting a rainbowed landscape.
A kaleidoscopic world created for all men,
and given to one man whose feats set him apart.
Whose courage raised him above.
At that point his life set an example for the world.
At the point where the blue of the sky,
And the blue of the ocean make a continuous
Pattern of here and beyond, small dots break the
Horizon's blend.
The sun
The moon.
The man.
In the minds of those who will aspire for
Greater things,
Lindberg still flies.

I tried to think of what I would have said,
If I'd been there when you left.

Don't go?
You shouldn't leave?
Thanks for being here?

I wonder what you would have said to me.
Or wouldn't either of us try to talk?

I think so.
Sad for those things never done?
Forlorn for those things left unsaid?
Regrets for those things left unfinished?
If we had touched, we would have said it all.
I guess I have to go now.
Goodbye.
See you.
Remember the good times,
And most of all. I love you.

Don't talk to me of yesterday.
Tell me what you'll do today.
Don't sit and dwell on what's gone by.
Plan instead for what you'll try.
Months and years will slip away
while you lament a bygone day.
Tomorrow a new peak you can climb
if you think about the pending time.

All of mankind went by the eyes of that beautiful little girl.
Eyes that sparkled with the dreams of a golden tomorrow.
She could climb on her father's lap for the strength of the world.
She could hold her mother's hand to touch the earth's beauty.
Those little eyes could see smiles,
and tears and joy and happiness.
They reflected so much that went by.
Every day the world looked so different.
She learned, she touched, she felt and she grew.
She grew to find the hurt of a world that's forgotten
What it's like to be a child.

If the page is blank when you're reading a book,
then write the next chapter yourself.
Kingdoms with soldiers, castles with moats,
Witches with cauldrons that boil.
Snow White, the woodsman, dwarfs and a queen
fighting their way through a maze.
Simple Simon, Jack be nimble, Polly, serve the tea,
Cinderella all alone, her slipper locked away.
Page upon page of fairy tales, of romance, love and hate.
take your pen and pencil to make the ending great.

The queen of hearts found the tarts,
the kingdom has been saved.
The prince fought through, the princess woke.
They up and rode away.
London bridge is standing strong, Humpty's on the wall.
The piper played a happy tune, the children danced and sang.

A fairy tale's a funny thing, filled with joy and laughter.

Work to write your book of life with happy ever afters.

We really have to give more time to loving.
We really have to give more time to concern.
We really have to give more time to caring.
We really have to give more time....
Of all our earthly possessions, time is one
of the most abundant.
Of all our earthly possessions, time is one
of the most precious.
To give of what we have in such quantities is
so inconsequential.
To give of that so valued is so magnificent.
Someone important needs time from you.
You need time from someone important.
We really have to give more time...

It was so tranquil I could hear drops of light
slowly sliding down moonbeams into the placid
Sea.
It was so quiet I could hear the twinkling of
Stars as they magically turned on and off at
the command of a celestial maestro.
It was so serene the breeze dared move the
elegant palms only to the gentle rhythm of the
sullen mood.
The low-flying gull knew not to destroy the
restful moment by doing other than the wistful
circling in the clear blue sky.
I had watched you walk toward me, and I reached
for your heart. Then, as I lay with you in
the splendor of the dream, I thought:
Is this wonderland wondrous because you are here, or
Are you here because you are a part of everything that's
Beautiful.

I've never seen anything more beautiful than
the rainbow pouring its colors into the
mountain greenery...except
I've never seen anything more peaceful than
the first flakes of snow gently settling in the arms
of a grassy field...except
I've never seen a more lovely sight than
the sun's brilliant rays playing off
the clear blue sea...except
I have never been more thrilled than at seeing
the mist of a cascading falls spread out
to accent the world around...except
I've never felt stronger than seeing the majestic tree budding
Before my eyes from the
Softly falling rain...except
I've never cared more
Than when I lifted that tiny baby bird
And saw it fly again...except

I've never loved more than
The view of a sky full of moon
And stars lighting the path
In a wonderful world...except
I've never seen anything more beautiful, peaceful
Or lovely...
I've never been more thrilled, felt stronger
Or cared more...
I've never loved more...
Than I've loved you.

How little the cost to be a friend.
The price is very small.
To answer to one in need
when one gives a troubled call.
A friend through good and bad times
is not an easy chore.
But to be a friend is a worthy role
and you never will be poor.

The old people walk down the street,
arm in arm, talking of what was.

The young people walk down the street ,
hand in hand, talking of what will be.
Only a few know they're young or old.
For the rest, it was, or it will be.
Hold the arm tight, squeeze the hand hard.
Savor the moment.
Tomorrow could be tomorrow.
Or today,
Or yesterday.

You can't expect the world to love if you don't.
You can't expect to be trusted if you don't.
You can't expect others to care if you're not
willing, also.
You can't expect to live in peace
if you're always looking for a fight.
You can't expect to give and take
if all you know is take.
You can't expect to hear the truth
if you live a life of lies.
Truth, trust, care, peace –
Smile, share, give, love.
Are you having a good day?

She rode in the heart
on the wave of a wish.
She sang only soft songs of love.
Her smile broke the bars.
She disguised how she felt.
She hid her cruel mission of life.
The lady in white was so happy that night,
For taking all you could give.
And she took.
The minstrel plays lonely refrains.

It seems our paths keep crossing
as we file through this life.
Each meeting a new place, a new
time and circumstance.
And then that path goes on with us.
Just for a moment be thankful
That these times happen.
That we can share.
That we can grow with this time together.
Then look forward with me to the next
time we meet, for it's the thought of those
special times, dear friend, that helps make it
all worthwhile.

When the wave has washed to shore,
will anyone care that it's gone for good?
When the moon has sunk into the sea
will anyone miss it on the horizon?
When the cloud has blown out of view,
will anyone miss it's billowy shadow?
When the cruelty of fall has taken the last leaf,
Will anyone revel in the tree's naked beauty?
Who will say that was a lovely flower
When the last petal has been crushed into the earth?
And when the reality of nature takes a man
Who will remember that he cared
And contributed
And tried
And loved.
To remember a little is to love
And the last petal was crushed.

You're a home, a vacation, a stop, a rest, a job.
The sailor from Massachusetts meets the tourist
from Connecticut across the piano bar.
The pretty girls walk down the street in twos and threes.
Followed by young men in fours and fives.
Ladies of the night shuffle slowly along
to the "sell your body" waltz.
While on the corner, vendors hawk their wares to the
melodious tones of a soft guitar.
Neons blink an enticing invitation to passerbys, urging them
to escape the reality of your cold streets.
Where the flickering light of TV sets is the only light
of houses, neatly spaced, in a row containing dwellers
slowly letting their existence flow away.
The mother rocks her baby, like a swaying tree,
teased by the breeze.
In the shadow of night, her soft figure casts a warm
glow of love to the world.
Yet, in the darkness of a field, an office, a factory,
the laborers for reason, for truth, for the wherewithal
to be here tomorrow.
You are a thousand different things
in a thousand different people,
all held captive in the chains of their experience.
Everyone together in your dark canyons. Alone.

Mom, where do little kids come from?
Wait till the next commercial, son.
Dad, let's go outside and play.
I'm watching TV right now. Go away.
We saw the funniest films about different zoos.
Don't bother your father during the news
I got straight As, Mom. The best in the class.
Huh? Oh, that's great, honey. Do you think you'll pass?
Can I take the car, Dad, I won't be late.
Will you please be quiet? This comedian's great.
Took a break from my studies to drop you a line.
I'll read the letter later. Just get channel 9.
If you came home more often it would sure make us glad.
Could you wait till the next commercial, Dad?

Consider the Sabbath.
The man who lives by his own book.
Writes his own commandments.
Worships his own God.
The lady that religiously sends
her kids to Sunday school.
Signs permission slips for religious
education and uses her God's name in
vain when they get home late.
The family that rushes their newborn
to church for baptism and then goes to
Church almost annually.
And, even on that one day, the dress, the
suit, even the shoes are more important
than the message.
The hypocrisy we live with.
See you in church on Sunday.
Have a nice dinner.
Happy holiday.

Soft ocean waves teased the beach
with a lover's caress.
Gentle summer breezes slowly moved
giant palms to a sensuous rhythm.
Quiet sounds of love rebound from
tropical air, saturated with the sadness of
time.
The early evening moon cast faint
shadows on the two in love.
As they walked hand in hand in the sand.
Past the old man watching the distant mountain,
he had so wanted to climb.
Maybe two can make it easier.
They stopped and as the waves,
the breeze, the sounds and the air
consumed their victims.
He cried.
And the mountain still hasn't been climbed.

Last year thousands visited the historic poppy fields of France.
That was World War I.
Last year thousands visited the Pearl Harbor monument in
Honolulu.
That was World War II.
Today I saw that sunken ship
with the men that gave their lives.
I thought of the futility;
each one should be alive.
Take your pictures, tourists
of the violent world's debris
but pray a moment as you leave
we won't have World War III.
The 38th parallel is now just another line on the students' globe.
That was the Korean War.
Saigon will soon be just another tourist stop.
That was the Vietnam War
The fighting still continues on
and mankind just won't learn.
If only war could stop for good.
if everyone would show concern.
Shrines are built for us to see,
and visit on our trips.
But let's build monuments of peace
and not for battleships.

Yesterday, I sat and watched the rest of
your life pass by.
I saw laughter and joy.
Tears and sorrow.
I saw people marching in and out
like little tin soldiers.
I saw time pass fast and slow.
Days so long you thought they would never end.
Days so short you wished they would never end.
There is love and want. Warmth and sharing.
I saw a life full of life.
I saw your whole life pass by.
But.
I didn't see me.

Walk along the beach today.
Everyman. lost within himself to celebrate the glory
that surrounds him.
Everyman, with names and images of the past walking with him.
Everyman, dreaming the beauty of a yesterday that was his today.
Everyman, hoping the good of a tomorrow will arrive early.
The sandcastle was just washed away and the child cried.
The adult stood firm against the pounding surf, knowing.
That which was destroyed can be built again, bigger, better
and resistant to the force that can destroy.
Let nothing stand in your way.
Build a better castle if you want it.
Or watch the old wash away, grain by grain, into the never
Relenting sea.

Goodbye is such a sad melancholy word.
Leaving is such a sad, foreboding time.
If streamers of paper could only hold us together.
If leis could only float forever along the shore.
A dream, a memory, a today, a tomorrow,
shattered by the harsh blast that reminds
of a destination far away.
There is no nice way to watch you leaving.
Even the soft sounds of gentle guitars
can never penetrate my tears.
Did you hear my heart shout love?
Did the pounding surf drown out my call to
come back?

Did today end the world of you and me,
or start a new world that we have to wait for?
I'll linger on the beach for a moment's thought
of you, then retreat to the solitude
of my loneliness to find what
the future will be.

The clouds drift by, never looking at the trees gasping for the
hidden sun
The river races on its course, committing massacre on
the helpless rocks
The stars draw their patterns in the dark sky, so distant their
glow won't illuminate.
The wind and rain trample the helpless shoots of a newborn
plant that will never give the pleasure of its bloom.
Even with its beauty, nature destroys.
And man, for all his care and concern, love and hope,
still follows nature.

The shops started to close. One by one.
The office buildings poured out their people
Laden with the fruits of their last minute shopping.
The last gifts had been bought, the last card mailed,
The last Merry Christmas shouted across the bustling street.
When the sun finally started to settle on the earth that's
wracked with pain and suffering, war and hate,
greed and lust, there was a hush.
A strangely unsettling peacefulness permeated
the air.
One day everybody smiled.
One day everybody greeted their fellow man.
One day everybody cared
One day everybody was at peace with the world.
What happens when the gifts are given and the tree is
untrimmed.
What a shame that Christmas eve is one day, Christmas is
Another.
And all the rest of the days blend into themselves.

The 617 rode on. A wistful kind of trip.
One looked out the window
and saw the self look back.
The kite seen sailing on its own
yet held down by a string.
The conductor readied travelers
for the next stop of the train.

The 617 rode on. A path of steel and iron.
It carried fright and love and want,
encased in streamlined frames.
A pitch black tunnel loomed ahead,
as well as fields of grain.
The conductor readied travelers
for the next stop of the train

The 617 rode on, entranced on moving fast.
The golden sun glared off the chrome
with heat that seemed intense.

The people riding ever on,
not knowing of the course
The conductor readied travelers
for the next stop of the train.

The 617 rode on, not knowing of the end.
The train of life took on its freight
to put in aisles of thought.
Quiet days and lonely nights,
and throbbing strong refrains.
The 617 rode on.
A courier to eternity.

An old man sat on the cold park bench
watching the world go by.
He sat, wondered and waited.
All left to answer was why.

For two score years he had been there
his future always blurred.
Not one chance ever came to him
his ideas were absurd.

A young man sat on the cold park bench
Watching the world go by.
He sat wondering and waiting,
yet to give life a try.

But when he looked in the old man's face
and saw himself much later, he saw the
old man's fear of life
The young man's seemed much greater.

I just can't let life pass me by,
day by day by day.
There's more out there than seen
From here.
Life cannot be that gray.

He got up from the old park bench
and walked across the green.
In search of opportunity
the old man had never seen.

Don't sit and wait for chances
the old man's face had said.
Seek out the way,
Seek out the sun,
and the path that's paved with gold.

Family

Today Is Mothers' Day

The first time I ever said "Thanks, Mom," it was probably for a candy bar- hers- that she broke off and gave to me.

I said thanks, through subsiding tears when she stopped whatever it was she was doing to make a scraped knee better with a Band Aid and a kiss.

I said thanks at birthdays and at Christmas.

I don't remember if I said thanks for the graduation gift. By then I was too old for that kind of thing.

It was Mommy- then Mom- or Mother. Even "the old lady" didn't escape her as a name.

I blushed when she tried to kiss me.

I was embarrassed when I was expected to respond to her "I love you" with the same.

And we both grew old.

Then that day I sat there in that same old chair, at that same old table, where she'd insist I sit until my asparagus was gone. She looked tired and worn.

I guess I did also.

It had been a long time.

"Are you taking care of yourself?" were the first words out of her mouth.

"Sure Ma. Got any coffee?" I said. She just smiled, and got me a cup of coffee.

She hadn't changed a bit.

I had.

I was back to saying "Thanks" again.

We visited for a while and I left. Not to run out and play. Or to go to school. Or to go off to my first job. Or the first date. Or to drive a car for the first time. Or to get married. Or to have my own child.

Those things were. And she was there.

But I went off to whatever tomorrow will be, with a kiss, and an "I love you."

I turned around and I kissed her, and I said, "I love you too, Mom."

I felt good when I said it, I wasn't embarrassed. I didn't blush. And, I meant it.

Then, kind of to myself, I also said, "Thanks, Mom, for the candy bar, and the Band Aid. For forgetting what time I got home late. For the food and clothes. And, even after all those were outgrown, for the love and care. The warmth and sharing.

Don't worry about me, Ma. I've still got all those things you gave me.

Today is Mothers' Day. She's sitting there smiling and telling all her friends what a wonderful child she has.

I'm sitting here telling you what a wonderful mother I have. It's a funny thing, that in all these years, I've never gotten around to telling her.

I've got to remember to do that, sometime.

The small child picked herself and her doll up simultaneously from the ground, to find a hand there to hold and feel for comfort. Funny how big that hand was, and how strong. Just beginning to walk; just starting to go her way, and he was standing right there.

He let go of the bicycle handles, stepped out of the way, and grinned from ear to ear while his son pedaled off, down the driveway, on his own.

Nobody saw the tear in his eye when he walked away from the school alone, after he registered a future valedictorian for kindergarten.

No man was ever more proud than when an awkward utility outfielder banged out a single in the Park Street little league.

He reached over and squeezed his wife's hand at graduation.

He stumbled, then quickly regained his composure, to walk straight and tall, as he escorted her to the side of another man, standing there and waiting to do all those things for her that he used to do.

"How in heaven's name can you always be that way, Dad?"

How did you always manage to do the right thing at the right time? Have the right words at the right moment? Have a smile when it was called for? A scowl when it was needed? A quarter for an ice cream…" Sacrifices for a college education? Good thoughts and much-needed encouragement whenever there was a rocky road?

Today I'm thinking about all those things that happened. All those good times we had, even when they weren't so good for you, but we never knew. Now, I know and when I close my eyes, I see an old man, bent over by the weight of time, harvesting memories from the garden of life he grew with the strength of kindness, and nurtured with love.

Even when you're tired, you're never tired of doing for those special people in your life.

Once I tried to tell you how much your being my father meant to me. All you did was chuckle, with that dismissive laugh you used so effectively to change the subject.

I can't try again to tell you, except in the way you taught me, my own way, that every single moment was worthwhile, and every day meant something to me, and I'm a better person for what you were. And, I know that's what you wanted.

So, Happy Father's day, just leave it at that, and I'll bet you a buck Baltimore wins the pennant.

The more time I spend around kids, the more fun they are. What I mean is, you can sure have a lot of fun just watching and listening to them... and in some instances, you don't even have to know who they are. For example, kids like the rest of us, are creatures of habit. They are also great imitators and whatever other kids do, they copy. For example, did you ever follow a school bus where every kid didn't stop at the mailbox on their way into the house... and how many of them have you ever seen find mail. Very few... but the fact that everyone else does it is enough to make everyone do it. Or, have you ever seen a bunch of junior high school age girls stand around for very long before they start practicing becoming cheerleaders. Drive by any junior high, almost anytime, and if there are more than two girls, they'll be jumping to strains of the school's fight song. Small children on the other hand are fun because they're just learning new words and new phrases. My oldest daughter for the longest time knew the family Italian dish: 'Quetti.' For as long as I could remember that was her way of saying spaghetti, and nothing could change her. My younger daughter loves the vegetable 'flower color' (cauliflour)... and she uses her toy wizzers to cut paper... And the fun thing is that no matter how hard we work at trying to correct her, it still comes out the same. I've heard other children mess up the English language in very funny ways... Many of which we wouldn't dare repeat here... But it was a great pleasure to arrive home the other day after my wife had been explaining my role at the radio station. From then on, I have been known as the radio station's boston... Even though most of the time I feel more like New York.

One of the quickest ways to go crazy is to stand in line with a little one waiting to sit on Santa Claus' knee. I had the opportunity the other day...all ready... and if I wasn't crazy before, that was enough to tip the scale. First of all, Santa should only spend about five seconds with each kid. What right has a child to tell Santa all the things he wants, while I stand in line... bouncing from one foot to the other... getting more and more impatient each minute, and wanting a cigarette desperately. That would be enough, but then there's this little kid in front, continually mistaking you for his father and running full steam into the front of your leg... while at the same time, the kid in back of you runs his stroller into the back of your leg... and your own child, impatient and anxious for the upcoming visit, just can't stand still. It gets so hot you take off your coat... which at the moment is just what you need... another something to carry. You slowly and steadily work your way almost to Santa Claus. You can just make out his beard and red suit in the distance. You slowly creep closer. You can now see the lines of age across his face. You're almost there... just a few ahead of you... you can see the happiness on the faces of the children as they climb onto his lap. You know that in no time your child will experience the same enjoyment... Just there in front of you... then two... then those words that bring trepidation to a parent's heart... "I've got to go to the bathroom."

Sparkling little eyes, wiping the sleep away, carefully edging around the corner to capture in that first moment the spectacle of a Christmas tree surrounded by all the fun and excitement asked for... begged for... prayed for over the course of the past few weeks. Promises of being good... well-intentioned promises, so hard to keep sometimes. Your whole life wrapped around the promise of a Christmas morning spectacular... and it comes true. As you see the toys, the fun, everything that you wanted laid out before your eyes... your whole life for the past several weeks culminating in that one moment... and poof... it's Christmas. This scene... or something similar was enacted in millions of homes around the world this morning... and even though every toy might not have been under the tree... and every wish wasn't fulfilled... There was something... something special for Christmas... something special... For this one day of the year. Christmas is something special. For those of us who can watch the job of holidays through a child's eyes are especially lucky... and I don't care how old you get... or how much you know... you'll always believe just a little bit that there's a Santa Claus... Even if your own eyes are just a little bloodshot from an evening of toy construction. Christmas is the most beautiful of all days... and it's because for me there can't be anything more special than watching the happiness of others...when I had a little part in it. Christmas is just beautiful... even if I have to wait one more year for my electric train.

I was bound and determined that I would be cool... maintain a dignified decorum... and act as natural as possible under the circumstances. I had told myself that when the time came, I'd take no more than the normal amount of cigarettes I carry... wouldn't pace the floor, but would try and be a comfort to my wife during her ordeal. Having a baby is not an easy task for anyone... but I knew there was more to it for her than me. We got to the labor room, and because the vigil was just the beginning we relaxed, she got ready, and we started to play cards. The doctor arrived and asked me to leave the room... which I did, retiring to the waiting room and the traditional role of fathers to be. Fortunately there were plenty of magazines because I had the opportunity to read them all... back to a 1955 copy of National Geographic. The dark and dreary of a late winter afternoon started to settle in outside so that the mood was changing, and so was mine... from anxious anticipation and slight nervousness. A couple people came by and visited for a minute and that helped relieve some of the tension. I went back into the labor room And, by now, things were happening and I could see that was no place for me to be. Back to the waiting room...Once I found myself pacing and sat down, somewhat disgusted that I broke my promise to myself... Read a couple of more magazines, was assured by the doctor that it wouldn't be long now... and watched the night pull its curtains on another day. Then seemingly at the moment I felt I couldn't wait any longer, I saw the doctor approaching. He was smiling... and God knows what kind of expression I had on my face. His hand was outstretched... said congratulations... it's a girl... everybody's good. Come this way and you can see them. Virginia finally arrived Monday. She sure was beautiful... so was her mother... as I saw them there together... and don't let anybody kid you... having a baby is as easy as two dozen magazines and three dozen cigarettes.

New times... And we'll talk about that...

We can put away the colored little walker with the plastic balls across the front. You won't need that anymore. If it was summer you'd be out romping around in the grass, but that will have to wait till a later date. Those little legs aren't quite sure enough to plow through the snow, though from the looks of you, you'd try it. By the time the snow is gone, though, you'll be able to join the acrobatic team on the swing set. That's the team with which your sisters keep going from sun-up to sun-down performing tricks that no sane adult would risk. Kids have so little fear, and you fit right into that category... Especially when you take off from your coffee table launching pad and pick up unbelievable speed as you head for the chair on the other side of the room, about halfway there sometimes those little legs run out from under the rest of your body. Frustrating, isn't it... so frustrating that sometimes following a nose dive or very unladylike plunk in the middle of the floor, you just have to sit there and cry... not because it has hurt your body, but your pride has been bruised almost beyond repair... or at least to the point where you have to be picked up and comforted for a moment... and given a little praise for the wonderful way you're moving around. Well, you deserve it... the praise... because it's hard for us to imagine how difficult it must be to make those little legs work that hard... and when you're having a hard enough time on a clear path, it's not funny at all when a toy gets in the way. After all, how are you supposed to know that you must step over it? Everything doesn't come at once. And remember last night when you got to the middle of the floor and did a complete 180 degree turn, and never even faltered. I told you what a good job that was... Now I don't have to keep you from crawling over to the cat's food. You can walk instead. We have literally hundreds of places that previously were inaccessible to you that now you can get to with that combination trot, waddle, wiggle, and walk. It's all very cute… it's one more step in growing up… it's walking for the first time… and isn't it fun for all.

Marching...

You always found your least faded pair of jeans...they were your best ones... contrasting to today's styles, when the more faded your jeans, the more likely they're your best pair. You got out your uniform shirt... the blue one with the long sleeves... and some Memorial Days those shirts were unbearably hot to march in... You made sure your badges were up to date... My mother's favorite line was... How can I sew it on when you don't even know where it is...? You got a ride, if you were lucky, to the street where the parade formed... and you were ready... A proud young cub scout ready to march what was an extremely long walk to the cemetery... there only to have to suffer through what for a youngster... and I suspect for adults, too, was an unbearably long-winded speech about things with which you had no comprehension. Such were my marching days in the cub scouts. Relegated to the back part of the parade... where you couldn't even hear the faintest strains of the high school band and thus were left to keep cadence the best way you knew how... which wasn't very effective... and which wouldn't have mattered anyway... because eight and nine-year-old boys have a hard enough time staying in line, let alone marching in step. Envied were the city officials who got to ride in the cars... I never understood why they got to ride... I still don't... and envied were the kids who were unaffiliated and who used the parade as an opportunity to decorate their bicycles with streamers and trail along behind. There were always a couple of people who rode their horses in the parade... and I always thought that if I was real nice to the man down the street that, come parade time, it would pay off... but it never did. His claim to fame was that he owned a convertible...and annually he was called on... and annually he responded with a well-shined vehicle for some faceless hand to use for waving from. Soon enough my marching days were over... I still love parades... the atmosphere... the excitement... and I do get a thrill when a well-trained unit follows a flag down the street... from my vantage point in a lawn chair... about three paces back from the curb.

The test... and we'll talk about...

It was one of the old sages, not Aristotle, but undoubtedly someone as worldly... who said something about the true test of fa-
therhood is sitting through your daughter's ballet recital when
the temperature is approaching ninety degrees. Well, I'm happy
to report that I passed the test... For yesterday I sat through
the recital that involved not only my daughter, but at least one
hundred other children as well... and survived to tell about it.
This wasn't my first experience with dance recitals. My oldest daughter initiated me early on and with two still younger,
it undoubtedly won't be my last. So yesterday's for Elizabeth,
the seven-year-old fell into the pattern that has now been es-
tablished. In our house we had a special occasion as well, with
grandpa and grandma visiting from San Francisco and able to
take in this monumental event with us. So needless to say the
whole experience took on special meaning. While it may be difficult for us, as adults, to sit without squirming for a very long
time, one can appreciate, and it helps the squirming, to know
that the one performance is the culmination of a full year's work.
Trekking to dancing lessons through rain, snow and all the other elements to learn the steps necessary for becoming a dancer,
and when the costume goes on, when the hair is fixed especially
for the big day, when the rehearsals and lessons are behind, the
dance recital suddenly is a big occasion. Mothers see their little
girls out on the floor and remember their first time. They see the
little girl as not being that little any more... and it brings a tear
to the eye. Even grandma sobs just a little bit. And almost as
soon as it began, despite the fidgeting, it's over. It's another first
and another experience in the book of life. So yesterday came
and went and the dance recital was a big success, and I learned
that while musicians have nightmares about their reed breaking

just before the solo, and baseball players tripping on their way home with the winning run, ballet dancers must agonize about the straps on their slippers coming undone, right in the middle of their beautiful dance.

What to do... and we'll talk about that.

It's part of the nature of children that they wait and wait for the day that school is finally out for the year. The newspaper always carries a picture of the kids rushing away from the school building as fast as their little legs will carry them. They are ready now to do all those things that they had to just think about as they sat in the dreary, boring classrooms. This euphoria lasts for a couple of days, maybe a week, and with an exceptional child, you might get through three or four weeks, but it is never any longer than that before the inevitable statement... there is nothing to do... is uttered by the youngsters. This applies generally to grade schoolers. By the time a youngster is of junior high age they either are capable of finding things to do... or don't care if they do anything. But here we are, now almost three full weeks from the end of school and it was only the other day that I heard the nothing to do pleas for the first time this year. Despite gallant efforts by various recreation departments to provide lots of things to do. Despite the fact that most yards you drive by are filled with swing sets and sandboxes, jungle gyms and slides. Despite the parents in this country who spend millions more for playgrounds. There is never anything to do. It has always amused me that we as a nation spend so much money on things not to do. I was reminded that as a youngster in grade school we lived in a house that had a huge old apple tree next to it. The tree belonged to a neighbor and there was maybe a length of a football field between the houses. That land he used for a mammoth garden. But he never plowed around the apple tree, and that was our sanctuary. My father installed a rope swing and the branches were low enough to the ground so that it was climbable, and in retrospect, and from a different perspective, now, I'm glad to think that when our "there is nothing to do" was answered with a "go play in the tree"... at least we weren't being forced to use some very expensive equipment.

There's something terribly exciting about preparing for a new baby. At our house we've been getting ourselves ready for the new addition for some time now. But it's only as the time gets really close that the father starts to feel anywhere near the anticipation that the mother has been experiencing for some time now. As the crib gets put up, and the layout of the layette engineered perfectly for ease and simplicity, or as much as possible. The fervor starts to mount. As the little tiny clothes start to come out and get out in just the right drawers, again for ease, you start to feel like the day is just around the corner… and of course it is. You might find yourself lying awake nights… wondering what it is that you're doing. Projecting the world, and yourself in ten, fifteen, even twenty years into the future. What kind of a world are you bringing a child into…? What if it's a boy… in ten years are you going to have the energy to go out and play catch after dinner. If it's a girl, are you going to have the patience to suffer through the trials and tribulations of another sandbox juliet. It all goes through your head, you look over at the crib, empty right now and know that in just a few weeks it will hold a little person that needs and wants love, caring, affection… Everything you have to give, every ounce of strength sometimes… every inch of patience sometimes… every bit of self-control sometimes… but always all your love. It's a little scary, it's a little worry, it's a lot of anticipation, and it's a lot of love. How many times have you heard of a woman say something to a man about the difficulty of having a baby. I understand, as much as I can, but you ought to try having a baby from a father's point of view… That ain't easy, either.

The hectic half hour... and we'll talk about that...

There was a time in my life when I was a part of some fairly involved television production, and this was back in the days when just about everything was done live. Not that I'm that old, it's just that the idea of taping programs isn't that old. Anyway, I used to call the minutes before one of these programs went on the air—a hectic half hour... For there were, seemingly, thousands of things that had to be done just before air time. When someone was climbing the ladders or a scaffold to move a light here or there... the talent would want to run through the teleprompter. The sound man would be stringing mic cords and the director would be checking his camera shots while some technician would inevitably decide that was the time to open the side of the camera for some adjustment or another. There were other things also, and if nothing else, that experience for those couple of years taught me not to panic, not to completely lose my cool, and to at least appear composed even if there was total turmoil inside. I learned those lessons well and have applied them numerous times over the years in a variety of situations. But I think I've finally found the time that it's not going to apply. And a new hectic half hour that may be my undoing. It's that time from 7:30 to 8:00 a.m. in our house... the minutes might be slightly different in yours... but just before everyone separates for their day's activities. Somehow coordinating breakfast, dressing, cleaning up, in general preparation for the day gets more complicated as the kids get older. I've gone to getting up a half hour earlier not so much because I like getting up- or get any more accomplished but just because I've found I can love the confusion after the second cup of coffee... and even my neat, even virgo mind, hasn't worked out a good system. The consolation is that with the TV programs, as soon as the show time was upon us, the confusion stopped. So come noon, I'm still trying to figure out why I poured orange juice on the baby's cereal.

Today… and we'll talk about that…

Today started just like every day has started for several months. Somewhere around 6:00 a.m. the baby woke up and woke me up. We have an unwritten deal that she'll do that every day. It works the other way also. If I should wake up first, as hard as I might try not to, my going downstairs is all she needs to awaken. She and I were joined about fifteen minutes later by the four-year-old, and as usual I read the paper while jostling with the two on my lap. We made the coffee, put out the cat, moving milk glasses off the paper. It seems the glasses always end up on the last paragraph of the story I'm reading. Maybe I should figure out a new way to read the paper, rather that laying it out on the table in front of myself. The seven-year-old joined us a few minutes later. I was happy to hear that even though she was going to wear her red sweater to school the teacher wanted them to wear coats. That helped avoid one argument. I lost count of the number of times I had to explain that, even though today is Halloween, we have to wait for tonight to go trick or treating… and no, it doesn't matter how much you eat, you still can't put your costume on right after breakfast. It was a typical day around our breakfast table. The topic might vary but the events and the characters all have the sameness, from day to day. And through it all, across the table, there is the smiling face of my wife. Somehow, as I grow more tired, she maintains a calmness. She keeps an order to the whole thing, and every once in a while she'll remind me that I took a particularly deep breath. If I breathe particularly deep, you can tell I'm approaching the edge of tolerance. Anyway, there is one thing different about today. It's our anniversary… and I mentioned all that happened this morning… and every morning, because it was just a few years ago that I was proclaiming my opposition to any kind of lasting relationship. Kids were out of the question, and so I knew the single life with late nights and late mornings, was made for me. How wrong I was then, how right it is now that the breakfast table is alive… and how even more right it is that she's there. She can diplomatically suggest to the kids that daddy's been the jungle gym long enough for a while. She's my business associate, and she's my confidant. She's my conscience, and confidence, she's my lover… and my friend. With her in mind a few years ago I asked a question that's still not answered… and bears repeating today… Is this wonderland working because you are here… or are you here because you're part of everything that's beautiful. It's just tough sometimes to verbalize these things when you're arguing that the raisins should go on the cereal, not the sugar donut.

For all the religious significance that there is to Christmas, and for all, even if the religious meaning is not there, there is a sense of enjoyment and fun that goes with the holiday season. But Christmas is also a time of tradition, and it was so last night as we decorated our Christmas tree. It would seem that we're one of the last ones to get the tree up, judging from all the lights and decorations I see as I drive around the area. But we decided when Ginny was born on December 15th that Christmas shouldn't start in our house before her birthday in order to be fair to her. Anyway, we got the tree up, and unburied the boxes of decorations that are carefully packed away every year, and went to work. Margaret, who's not quite two, really participated for the first time. Needless to say, if you were concerned with just a smoothly flowing operation, three kids and two adults all trying to do as much as they can doesn't help… But if you're concerned with meaning, the room was full of it. Most of our decorations are homemade. There are styrofoam balls with glitter, paper cut outs and seemingly hundreds of other pieces all made with more than just material. All made with love and meaning. There are some store bought ornaments, there are some with each person's name engraved on, there are some that are carefully sewn, and of course, layers and layers of tinsel. The point is, though, that our Christmas tree is an annual reminder, at least to my wife and me, of past years. She's very good at being able to remember when a decoration was made. On some she has attached a special meaning, and as tradition would have it, in our house, we always play Christmas music on the stereo while the tree decorating is under way. Just to add to the atmosphere. There are also scattered around our house lots of other homemade decorations, creative in their appearance, creative in their construction. To look at them today, you'd never guess what spare parts of odd things went into their building. If you're not into the decoration-making, you miss a good deal of the fun, and the meaning of Christmas. And I'd suggest that right now, this week, you find time to make a few things that you could still use this year, and have to put out next year... You'll be surprised how much it can add to your holiday season.

The steps seemed a little longer. Every year they seemed harder to climb, but you could never remember them as difficult to get up as they were today. You went in her room, weaved through stacks of sweaters over there, slacks over there, shoes spread all over the place, some drawers of her big dressers open, books in a zig zag pile on the corner of the night stand, ready to topple at the slightest breeze...But through it all you went and sat down at the foot of her bed. There was a suitcase, a high school graduation gift, opener and partly full, taking up most of the bed. A couple of stuffed animals, reminders of the days that now seem so long ago, rested on the pillow... and on the floor a new trunk. Brimming over with clothes, records, the new blanket, and on top the radio, the one with the abominable music that played through home, work, sleep, reading, relaxing... every time she was in the house. How quiet it was now with the cord neatly wrapped around its light pink plastic frame. Selected so carefully to match the rest of the room. You noticed your picture was not on the dresser. Undoubtedly packed away for the trip. That was nice, but so was the picture of her latest steady, the one with long hair and the loud car. That's not so nice. "I'm almost done," seemed like hardly the appropriate salutation for such traumatic times. But today, of all days, you'd let it, and simply respond with "that's good, because we've got to leave soon." And you sat there watching as the piles on the floor got smaller and the suitcases and trunk overflowed. The eyes of that stuffed tiger, on her bed every day since she was two, looked as sad as yours as you sat there. You saw again the first day she walked... remembered how you cried when she went off to kindergarten the first time... You vowed to look in the basement for the violin you were sure she could perfect... and the guitar she was sure she could master. You'd sat right where you are now for that first serious talk; you never could get all the poster paint out of the carpet. A reminder of her campaign for class president, and in the corner of the closet stood the crutches, memories of a most expensive ski trip she took two winters ago. The top on the trunk slammed down, bringing you back to the moment. You looked up, saw a smile on her face as she dabbed your eye with a tissue. And said, "I'm growing up, but I'll be home for Thanksgiving." It sure will be quiet now... the house will be easier to keep clean... you'll have another reason to watch for the mailman. And the steps will continue to seem harder to climb... But they'll never seem longer than that day your little baby went to college.

Today was garbage day. I cleaned out the refrigerator of leftover food that had been there for a couple of weeks. I was cleaning it out to make room for more food that we would be throwing away in a couple of weeks. Three- or four-days' worth of meals disposed of because it was leftovers.

I took the bag of garbage to the receptacle that would go to the curb, and in doing so I walked past the car parked in the drive-way — the car that we use for a myriad of purposes. It takes us shopping, it takes us to football fields and gyms, schools, and of course to go buy more food. It takes us to softball and base-ball games, we go to movies, to the circus, the parades and con-certs, not to mention to parties. Never once have we had to dig through our pockets to find change for gas money to get to any of those places. Never once have we had to move our belongings out of the way so we could sleep. No. We slept in our comfort-able house with hot air in the winter, and cool air in the sum-mer. The comfortable house with large TVs, chairs, couches, big plush beds, and clothes pouring out of the closets. Never in our lives have we had tomorrow's clothes in a big bag stuffed in the bottom of a cart with our few other belongings.

I looked around and saw rows of neat homes with green grass and bushy trees. People were washing their cars and kids were drawing hopscotch courts in the driveway. I did not see any doorways with people hovering over their few possessions.

No. I saw comfort hovering. I saw happiness hovering. And, I saw garbage cans lining the street, all full of leftover food and discarded cans and bottles and wrappers representing instant gratification for a seemingly insatiable hunger. I do not know hunger. No one I know experiences hunger. I will keep throwing away food every week or so. I will be snug in my tiny little corner of the world.

And, every time I go to the garbage can, I will be thankful.

Requiem for a graduation.

How sad that there are millions of young people around the world who will never experience the rite of passage from secondary education to the real world. How anticlimactic to arrive at the end of the quest and there is no one or nothing there to collectively celebrate the completion of years of work. Years of aiming for the goal to complete a life phase.

Graduation is students standing on shore and looking out at a huge body of water. A few will get the edict to sink or swim. But for most, the assembled family and friends, relatives, and acquaintances from all over the globe stand with them on that shore as they look out at the horizon. There will be luxury yachts for some. Houseboats for some. Military ships wait for many. There are powerful motorboats, little rowboats, canoes, kayaks, even the surfboards waiting for a few. But each student, buoyed with the support of their collected "fans," head out into the ocean we call life.

However, this year it is going to be lonesome standing on that shore by yourself. You will still get the life jacket, but not with a presentation flourish. You will still be loved and praised for all you have accomplished so far, but time does not stand still. Without hearing the cheers and shouts from the shore, get in the boat, mighty warrior, and cast off for a life of meaning. And please make it calmer than what you are sailing into.

100,000 Americans have given their lives to Covid

That is more than the 33,606 men and women who gave their lives in the Korean conflict

That is more than the 58,318 men and women who gave their lives in the Vietnam War.

These people didn't leave this country with guns and bayonets.

These people didn't leave their hometowns.

These people fell victim to an unseen enemy and the people who could not or would not acknowledge its terrible dangers.

If you failed to social distance, wear a mask, complained because you couldn't wander around a store or a shopping center, go to a ballgame or swim in a public pool, you have a share of those deaths on your being.

I sit here tonight with a tear on my cheek. Not because of any one individual, but for society that has again said we don't care about how many die, or how many are left to mourn.

We care about ourselves, our selfish selves, and worship the mantra: if it doesn't affect me it can't be that bad.

Rest in peace, you 100,000 friends, neighbors, and loved ones who got caught in the attack of ignorance and indifference to fellow man.

I keep hearing so many people say, "I just can't wait to get back to normal."

I keep asking myself what they are going to get back to. What is normal?

Every time our society has experienced an event that affected millions of people, we have bounced forward. Society does not bounce back. It never has. I don't think it ever will.

After illness events, we have put the events behind us and gone forward. Sadly, not learning as much as we should have from them.

After wars, we mourned our losses, celebrated our victories, and moved forward. And we prepared for more.

After major impacts on our way of life, we change our way of life and move forward. The stock market crash of '29 comes to mind, yet, not that many years later, greed again reared its ugly head.

If you were born after 2001, going through airport screenings, going through metal detectors in public buildings, having to be "buzzed into schools" and Homeland Security are all "normal."

So, what I am trying to say is normal will be what life is like after tomorrow… or the next day.

Normal changes from day to day. Sometimes from hour to hour.

When you go back to work, go back to school, or try and resume a regular routine in your life, that will be the normal of the moment.

What you really should be saying is, "I really don't like today's normal very much and I am anxious to try tomorrow's normal."

But don't expect that tomorrow's normal will be like today's, or yesterday's, or last week's or year's.

It has always been that way. Normally we don't think about it.

I don't know if every family has a Gladys and Oca. But we did.

Gladys was Grandma Grace's sister, and Oca was her husband.

They lived in the same town as Grandma Grace and Grandpa Bert and they were all very close.

Back in the mid-forties, after the war was over, Christmas was really special. The brothers, sons, fathers, and husbands in our family all got home. The only exception was my dad, who was injured on Guam and spent a year and a half in various military hospitals. But this Christmas, even he made it home.

Home for us was Grandma Grace and Grandpa Bert's during the war.

But, this one Christmas, and the last one I remember at that house, my mom and dad, my brother Billy and I were there.

So was my mom's sisters Aunt Dorothy and her husband Uncle Stubby, Aunt Margarite and her husband Uncle Harry, and her brother Uncle Donald with his new wife that he met and married while stationed in England. Aunt Betty, for whatever reason, became my favorite for years and years and years.

There was also Aunt Vera. She was Grandma Grace and Aunt Gladys' sister.

IT was a houseful. My brother, Billy, and I were the only young people.

All the brothers and sisters and cousins would soon be on the way. Our family's contribution to the boomers.

Anyway, everyone was staying at the big, and I mean big, old house on Church Street...

Except for Gladys and Oca.

When Christmas morning arrived, Billy and I went downstairs with our youthful excitement. There were lots of presents under the tree, and in checking the tags, we knew some were for us and some presumably were from Santa Claus.

We retrieved our stocking that was hung by the chimney and found as was expected: an apple, orange, a few walnuts, a few pecans, and the annual filbert. There was probably a toothbrush also, but I don't remember that.

We were grateful, of course, because fruit in Upstate New York in December, any year was precious, but these last few years even more so.

But now, we had to get to the presents under the tree.

But NO... we had to wait for Gladys and Oca.

Why don't you go and have some cereal?

Why don't you go outside and play in the snow for a while?

Why don't you go upstairs and read to each other for a while?

Why don't you go in the kitchen and see if you can help Vera start breakfast?

Why don't we grow up and graduate from college? I think we will have time.

Finally, seemingly hours later, Gladys and Oca arrived, joyful and chipper. They had no idea what torture they had put us through and, of course, I wouldn't tell them.

Now, don't get me wrong. Gladys and Oca were wonderful people. I mean that. they were kind, loving, and generous.

But my longest-lasting memory of that Christmas was waiting and waiting and waiting for Gladys and Oca.

Hello God.

It's me. We are all getting together for Thanksgiving and I thought it would be good to share a couple of thoughts with you before we eat.

First of all, thank you for all of us being here together again this year. Every moment we get to spend as a family is precious to me and I think the rest of the family as well.

This is the first ask. Look over all the members of our little group going forward as we all try to make sense of some of the craziness going on in the world, face our own personal challenges, and try our best to be supportive of all around us. Give us the strength to face those challenges and come out on the other end as better people, more able to help make ourselves and those around us better in the process.

We ask that you look after and give strength to all those who have been affected by the terrible, terrible disasters that have befallen us this year. The earthquakes, hurricanes, floods, fires, tornadoes, and even the flowing hot lava that have ravaged people, even entire communities and left them with just a belief and a hope that things will get better. Please make that so.

Give strength to the men and women who have been called upon to provide relief for those stricken by tragedy. Firefighters, police officers, doctors, nurses, and the myriad of others who give so unselfishly of themselves to try and alleviate some of the pain of others.

Give an extra little looking-after to the men and women who

will be away from home this Thanksgiving as they protect our country from real and perceived enemies of our way of life.

Maybe you can give a shout-out to other members of our family and our friends who dwell in our hearts and minds today and every day but are not at our table.

Anyway, you have a lot of others to attend to and we want to eat so let me just say thank you for your love and guidance for us all.

Love, Your buddy Don

Hi God. Don here again with the family as we gather for our Christmas Eve dinner.

We all made it through another year and for that we are eternally grateful.

As special as every year is, this year brought a lot of changes which we celebrate.

Kaity found a new career and a new job. Renee continues to dazzle at Amazon. Lexie moved to a new school and our workaholic, Hannah, continues to perform on top at school and hold down two jobs. All this while Dan left elementary school behind and moved to middle school.

Please continue to look over them as we proudly watch them grow into magnificent citizens of the world.

Watch over Uncle T and Uncle Ray as their work calls them more and more away from home and family. May they simultaneously be successful fathers and husbands.

Watch over Ginny and Mag as they continue to perform their jobs on a super high level as trusted, loyal employees in their fields and on the home front as loving caring wives and moms.

Look out for Liz as she searches for the next plateau in her life. Give her the wisdom to see right from wrong for herself and her family.

As for the Hum and I… we thank you for every day.

Every time we wake up, even at 3:00 a.m. in the morning, we

are grateful for one more day with our loved ones. Truly we are blessed.

Please look out for other friends and special family members who may be suffering setbacks in their lives. Please help them heal and be full again.

Look over military and first responders that keep us safe every day.

And finally, thank you for the here and now. That we can look to each side… we can look across from ourselves and we can see the family that makes this whole adventure so worthwhile.

And as I know you are there for us, so do I know that almost every person at this table is there for every other person. Grant us the strength, individuality, and collectivity to wend our way through the obstacle course we call life.

And Oh, Merry Christmas and tell Jesus happy birthday.

Love,

Don

The other day I heard a young man say, "I don't believe in Santa Claus anymore."

I said, "That's okay if you don't want to believe. I still do."

And that's what we are talking about today.

It's alright to believe whatever you want to believe. Of course, there are some caveats. You shouldn't believe in something that will harm someone else, or an animal, or the earth.

I believe that tomorrow morning, the sun will rise, giving us light and warmth.

I believe that tomorrow evening, the moon will rise over the horizon.

I believe in the strength of family. The family, when given the opportunity can help each member grow and flourish way beyond their individual efforts.

I believe that tonight, a baby will be born that will change the world.

No, not the baby in the manger. That happened and that's really what we should be celebrating, but this baby will be born in a sterile hospital room, or another not-very-desirable location.

But, just like the babies born every yesterday, I believe every baby can and has changed the world somehow.

So maybe you don't believe in the fur-lined red suit, flying reindeer, and North Pole toy workshops.

That's your choice.

But you can believe that someday you will tell youngsters that Santa Claus is on his way.

And then they will say, 'I don't believe in Santa Claus,' and I hope you will say, 'Maybe Santa doesn't wear a red suit, and his name is not just Santa Claus. He has lots of names.'

It's mom, dad, sister, brother, aunt, uncle, cousin, grandmother, or grandfather.

And, it's not just the presents under the tree.

Those people all bring you a more special gift.

Their gift is to give you a chance. The chance to be all you can be.

And for that, give thanks.

I'm the Grandma that got hit by flying longhorns,
Coming home from Ginny's Friday night.
I was actually on my way to visit Maggie,
When flying hooves and horns came into sight.

I jumped on one and rode round the city,
Taking in the sights as best I could.
But heaven knows you can't enjoy the beauty,
When riding on a pile of ribeye steaks.

They dropped me off in time to visit daybreak,
And dodge the flying paper delivery.
I went to bed and thought about my evening,
With visions of the sights that I'd just seen.

Now you know that Grandmas don't tell stories,
So, believe me all I've said is very true.
And remember if you venture out to neighbors,
Come home before you get past 1:00 or 2:00.

The other day, someone asked me (Hannah, to be specific) some very thought-provoking questions, which is not unusual on our way to school.

The first question was, "Did you have a role model when you were growing up?" That was easy: my mother. For all the reasons you would call someone a role model. Always supportive, loving, never judgmental, and always living her life in a way that could be an example of a kind, generous, and thoughtful person. And, she made a mean chocolate cake. I answered that question right away...

The second question was a lot more difficult and took a lot more time to think about. "In your long life, Bumpa, what is the most important lesson you have learned?" You go ahead and pick out one most important lesson. It's not easy.

After trying to narrow down an awfully long list of life lessons, I got two. A close second was to Never Lie.

Number one: Life is never just about you

No matter what you say, no matter what you do, no matter how you act or react, you are going to have an effect on someone else.

Normally I would not share a random granddaughter conversation, but today it's particularly timely because I can't think of another group of people who embody the spirit of making it about others more than mothers. And, being that it's Mother's Day, on behalf of every son and daughter that has walked the face of this earth, thank you for being a mom. For being supportive; for being loving; for being an example of kindness and thoughtfulness. Thanks for being Mom and we love you. Wear the title Mom with the same level of pride that we have when we say, "my mom."

HAPPY MOTHER'S DAY

When you are a young boy growing up in upstate New York, your exposure to baseball is limited. As a player, you get to ride a school bus once a week to a nearby city to play in a recreation league for the summer. You can go on Sundays to the high school field to watch the "town team" made up of college students home for the summer and local athletes still searching for the last glimmer of glory, and when you get older, you can play on the high school team where the most glorious thing was wearing your uniform to class on the afternoon of away games so you could take the bus before school was out to get to the game.

So, when our family (all seven of us) made our bi-annual Griswold-type trip to my uncles in Silver Springs, Maryland, that was an adventure in and of itself. The year 1953 is forever etched in my memory. Not quite 13, I found out upon arrival that Uncle Bob had tickets to a Washington Senators game. But not any baseball game; a professional baseball game. And, not just to see any team; we were going to see the Yankees.

That was going to be the best day of my life, rivaled only by when my grandparents showed up one day with new bikes for my brother and me.

The Washington Senators were not a particularly good baseball team. They were actually a bad team, but that did not matter because we were going to see them play the Yankees.

I don't remember the score. I don't remember what the stadium looked like. I don't remember if our seats were any good. But I was at a "big league" game. And, the one thing I remember was etched in the sports portion of my brain to this day: BILLY

MARTIN STOLE HOME. Did you see that? He stole home. Never even challenged. You can't do that. But he did.

In the subsequent 63 years of my life, I've seen great teams in person. I've watched games in some of the most legendary stadiums of major league baseball. I can't tell you very much about any of the games or much about the stadium, but I still remember BILLY MARTIN STOLE HOME.

As a youngster you go through hundreds, probably thousands of experiences, and while you gain something from most of them, there are few that remain in your mind like a photographic image. And as you get older, there are some of those remaining that tend to drift away until what's left of your childhood is just a vague recollection of those days. Such is the case of my life, and there are few of those vivid images left, yet there are a couple I know I will never forget.

Just as clear as if it were yesterday, I see a young family standing on a railroad station platform: a mother, father, and two young sons, one about three and one a little over a year old. The old steam locomotive type pulls into the station and stops. The father, as handsome as any man ever was in his navy officers' uniform, hands the youngest son to the mother, then bends down and picks up the older son for a hug and to remind him to help Mom. An embrace for the mother and then onto the train and off to war.

The next period of time is that vagueness of sitting in dark rooms during the blackouts with the radio talking about things no youngster understood. I can again vividly remember that day I saw the naval officer again and even with warnings to not touch daddy's head, a youngster's curiosity couldn't be stopped, for he didn't look the same as when he left. It wasn't until many years later that I could understand that the scar across his head was just the surface of the scars of war inside that never would heal completely. I guess the point of all this is that you don't necessarily have to be a veteran to appreciate those that are, and to remind ourselves that even if times, transportation, or the people are different, there are much prettier things for youngsters to engrain in their minds forever than a father going off to war.

There are times when you go into instant shock. Those times when you are sure the worst has happened, and before you even know the circumstances, you start to get prepared. For example, the phone ringing in the middle of the night. Nine times out of ten it's a wrong number, but you are still ready for the worst. Or, when the boss walks by and says something like "see me before you go home tonight." Your day is going to be ruined because you are sure today is the day you get fired. Or, how about when one of the kids come running into the house screaming for Mommy at the top of their lungs. You are sure one of the neighbors' kids has run over somebody with the tricycle. Or the one tossed offhanded to me by my wife. "You know what I did in the supermarket?" That simple little line delivered in a profoundly serious voice sends chills up the spine. What happened in the supermarket? She picked up the butchers' cleaver and threw it at him? She knocked down the stock boy's newly formed fifty level pyramid of canned peas? A whole shelf of condiments got tipped over and she laughed as the clerk faced a swirling sea of mustard, ketchup, and mayonnaise? She filled up several carts and picketed the cashier lines to protest high prices? The worst went through my mind. Surely, she was banned from the supermarket forever. Whatever it was, the embarrassment when the news hit would cause us to hide in shame. But, regardless of what it was, I wanted to know. I had to know. I was now prepared. My adrenalin was pumping, my heart beating rapidly, perspiration beaded my brow. I said, "What did you do at the supermarket?"

"I squeezed the Charmin." She squeezed the Charmin? For that I almost had a heart attack. "I got caught too," she said. "A lady saw me, and I was so embarrassed that I put it in the cart and bought it."

"Wonderful," said I, barely able to restrain myself, but in the face of all, I kept my composure. You know what I did today? I came this close to throwing these mashed potatoes in your face.

I don't think too much about the idea of leaving children un-attended in a car while adults run into the store. It happens more often than you might think, according to a survey I have conducted myself. You can drive into any shopping center parking lot or through downtown almost any time the stores are open and find at least one or more children pretending to drive, sticking their heads outside of the windows, or even hopping in and out of the car like it was a revolving door. I'm sure that at one time or another we have all heard of the acci-dents caused by well-meaning kids who accidentally released the emergency brake, or kicked the car out of park and had it roll away with them in it. More often than not, the fun turns to tragedy, and in a matter of seconds. In other words, even for a minute, it's not a good idea. If you have the kids with you, take them into the store. Or, don't go into the store. Or, expect an accident.

Or, things can go as I saw happen the other day. This very nice lady came out of the store with her arms filled with the fruits of her shopping. Reaching under the bags, she tried to open the door of her car with two children inside. The door wouldn't open. You guessed it; the young kids had locked their mother out of the car. In a very pleasant voice, I heard her ask them to unlock it, which they did not. Still calm, but a bit more hurried, she told them that she loved them very much and asked again to unlock the door, which they again did not. The packages were beginning to feel heavy. More irritated now, she told them to open the door. The kids thought it was a wonderful game. They didn't open the door. The woman shouted some obscenities at the children, but the door still did not open. Finally, out of frustration and exhaus-tion, she sat the bags on the ground. She fumbled through her purse, found her keys, opened the door, and said something to the effect that the children were in for it. No question the kids were wrong, but so was leaving them in the car. Another example of two wrongs making a fight.

Fall brings changing leaves, cold weather, rain, and the new edition of The Farmer's Almanac. I'm happy to report that this year is no exception. For the 184th year, The Farmer's Almanac is, I would guess, the most well-known publication in existence, and probably for its weather forecasting. It's hard to think of a time when a serious discussion on weather occurs, that at one time or another, someone doesn't mention what was said in The Farmer's Almanac. I'm as interested in the weather as the next person: I took my complimentary copy and tried to figure out what the weather would be for the next year on several key dates: my birthday, Fourth of July, Labor Day, and other holidays, but it's more interesting for me to look at the ads. As the saying goes, you just can't hardly find them anymore. Not the ads, but the kind of ads. What other magazine or annual do you know of that within the span of a few pages is going to sell you a lucky genie cast, 100% cowboy boots, life insurance for burial expense, false teeth, and genuine World War II helmets? There of course is a wealth of genuine information in The Farmer's Almanac, and plenty of interesting reading, with this year being perhaps more interesting than some others, being that it is the special bicentennial issue. But all in all, it's fun to have around, and each year is certainly a collectors' item. Did you know that to rid your room of smoke, soak a towel in water, wring it out, and swish it around the room. That is one of this year's ten best household hints. They neglected to tell you that swishing a wet towel around will also get rid of any smokers in the room. For those who might be planning a surprise birthday party for me, the weather is supposed to be nice. The Fourth of July is supposed to be nice also, but if you've got anything planned for March 14th, forget it. We're going to have a blizzard, or so it says on the page just before the buried treasure finder ad.

I took the time the other day to check around in several television stores and I found that every set in stock was manufactured with an on/off switch. That probably doesn't come as a surprise to any of you, but I was beginning to wonder. What promoted my curiosity more than anything else was all the discussion taking place around The Family Hour, and what can and cannot be shown. The Family Hour is, as best I can determine, the first hour of prime time each night plus one hour preceding. The television industry had determined, upon apparent heavy prompting from Washington, that nothing can be aired in that time which would be acceptable to anyone over the age of ten. Again, our leaders, government, and industry have determined that no one has any intelligence. What topped it off for me was a recent decision to not allow the Venus de Milo statue to be shown on The Cher Show because her navel shows. Now, how many children do you know that don't know about belly buttons? Or how many adults do you know that would be offended by a legitimate piece of art? Or more importantly, how many people do you know that have a TV set without an off button? Personally, I'm getting tired of being fed what appeals to the intelligence of a fourth grader. Controversial topics can be presented entertainingly, and people will watch it. All in The Family and Maude are two good examples of that. If there is a program that might offend me or I don't like, I don't watch. I am not so dumb that I can't find other means of entertainment when television is no good. I read books, I play cards, I write poetry and short stories. I play Ping-Pong, I do woodworking, and play with my daughter. I listen to the radio, play the records, and change the channel. I talk to the wife, I might even fall asleep on the couch, but most importantly, I exercise my freedom of choice. Let's keep interesting programs on the TV, let's not censor, and let's keep making television sets with the on/off switch. That is all we really need.

Richard Bach is, of course, best known for his book, Jonathan Livingston Seagull, but he wrote another book about his adventures as a barnstormer, and that was brought to mind the other day while taking one of our weekend trips. We were traveling down a four-lane highway, just slightly exceeding the speed limit when a sheriff was spotted, presumably ready to take off after the next speeder... presumably me. I gradually eased down speed trying to not look panicked as we drove past the distinctly marked vehicle, checked him in the rearview mirror, saw he wasn't following, and breathed a sigh of relief. Before the sheriff was out of view, there appeared to be cars pulled off the shoulder up ahead. I expected a neatly uniformed man to step out, signal me to pull over, and courteously tell me that I had been clocked in the radar, but no such thing happened. Instead, the cars on the side of the road increased in speed as both sides were now crowded, and everyone was craning their necks skyward for a glimpse of something that I was unaware of at the moment. Being curious, I too pulled over at the first opening I could find on the shoulder, and I craned my neck skyward also. After several minutes of looking with a now-stiff neck, there suddenly appeared to be something rising from a field about a half mile away. A three wing airplane followed shortly by a two wing airplane, both brightly painted and both above the vintage of World War I. Thereafter, for as long as we decided to watch, these two old planes chased each other around the sky, grazing the tops of trees and each other. It was fun for a while, but eventually left several hundred people still parked along this road, watching these modern-day barnstormers perform. I doubt that it was Richard Bach and a friend, or Snoopy and the Red Baron, but whoever it was, my thanks for entertaining me, my family, and the sheriff.

I sat talking to my wife about leaving the pumpkin on the front porch and what the odds were that it would get smashed or stolen before Halloween, and naturally, my mind drifted back to those dark cold Halloween nights of my childhood. One could never accuse us of not having fun, but on the other hand, none could ever call us destructive... well, almost no one. There was that one Halloween when we located a garden with an ample supply of tomatoes rotting on the ground, and rather than shoot them, as any innocent bystanders, we preceded to get into a fight amongst ourselves. There were several Halloweens when a candy salesman lived up the street from us and we managed to trick or treat his home several times, each time receiving an ample supply of treats. There were the usual boyish pranks like jumping out of the bushes to scare a group of unsuspecting girls, but the most disturbance we caused was to a couple of elderly ladies who threatened to call the police if we ran across their backyards one more time. When we were noticeably young, trick or treating was confined to the immediate neighborhood, or maybe the home of your parents' friends several blocks away, and only because they wanted to see how cute you were in your costume. I suspect that not much has changed, but those that seize upon the opportunity to be vicious, those who find it necessary to bus their children to the most populated areas in the city, and those that would do genuine and permanent harm to innocent children with treats, have all contributed to making Halloween a more dreaded than happily anticipated holiday for all. My pumpkin will stay on the porch. If someone wants to break a little girl's heart by smashing our pumpkin, then help yourself. But watch out because I may be hiding in it.

There is nothing more rotten than having a cold. I don't mean the real bad cold where you are laid up in bed, or so serious that you're fearful of complications, I'm talking about the runny nose type of cold. You feel perfectly fine, like you could go out and do twenty laps with the best of them, that is, if there's a pocket in your gym suit to carry your handkerchief. Usually the runny nose type of cold won't respond to any remedies, at-home or purchased, and they make you sound a lot worse than you really are, so there is little to do. My favorite remedy for colds is a few shots of a very strong alcoholic beverage, perhaps mixed with a little honey, though that part is optional. I have tried several times for several days in a row to get rid of a cold by this method. I'll have to admit that like everything else, it doesn't work for me, but I did find myself not minding the cold very much, the more Jack Daniel's treatment I indulged in. Another problem with the runny nose type of cold is that you rarely get any kind of sympathy from anyone. If you are really sick, people are more than willing to extend little courtesies to you. Even a bad cold will at least get you a simple "how are you feeling?" but a runny nose and stuffed head usually gets nothing but uncomplimentary glances from everyone around you every time you sniffle or excuse yourself to blow your nose. Being sick is never any fun, but being sick, and I use the word advisedly, with a runny nose is an absolute bore. So, the next time you see a poor little kid with a runny nose, give them a little sympathy and be thankful it's no worse. After all, they could have a moustache.

A year ago, my family sat down on Thanksgiving with about 25 friends whom we had invited to join us for dinner. It was a yeoman's task presented to my wife to prepare dinner for that many people, and even as exhaustion got to her as the last of our visitors lingered on into the evening hours, we were grateful for the wonderful people who were with us. The people were from work, people we occasionally saw, saw often, but all of them friends. It was one of those mixtures of people that you would probably never believe could even be in a room together without something short of a World War III bomb shelter, but all were there cramped in a small apartment enjoying each other and the fellowship that a holiday can prompt. I could look around that room and in the instance of every single person, give you at least one reason why they shouldn't be thankful. Lives of sadness for some of them, moments of sadness for all, days of loneliness yes, and hours of depression sure, but for that moment they were together and genuinely enjoying it. There was not sadness, there was no loneliness. There was laughter, there was fun, there was a feeling of togetherness. People of all races, religions, political persuasions. Old people, young people, even a couple of kids, but everyone was there because we wanted them there and they wanted to be there. In one short year I have lost track of some of those people, I've met a lot of new people, and I've had several new experiences. I have lots to be thankful for and I am, but forever I will remember the day I sat down for dinner with the world, and no one noticed we forgot the cranberry sauce.

Prose

It scares the devil out of me to go to the supermarket. It's bad enough to have to cope with the cart jockeys who weave in and out between rows of shelves. It can be a physically traumatic experience to have to switch between being too hot and too cold, depending on whether you are in frozen foods or canned vegetables. It can be frustrating to get caught behind a comparison shopper who moves at the pace of a snail. It's difficult, if understandable, to be in a store on stock days, when the rows are piled high with cartons and it's just downright rude of the people who use their trips to the market as a social experience. Three carts abreast, women will wind their way down the aisles, blocking all behind them and throwing oncoming shoppers into a hasty retreat. The worst part of that is that usually in each basket it's just one item, and usually it's a loaf of bread. It hurts to have a cart run up on your heels by a misbehaving child, and I have waited up to half an hour while someone pays for twenty-five dollars' worth of groceries with pennies and nickels. But the one thing that scares me, the one thing that actually causes me physical fright, is to be casually shopping, minding my own business, watching out for other shoppers, pushing my cart slowly around the corner and be confronted by a lady in curlers. Not ordinary curlers, but those great big things big enough to drive a Tonka truck through. I always feel embarrassed, like I've walked into the woman's house, which is where curlers should be worn. Those same women who wouldn't be seen dead without a fancy coiffure at a drive-in restaurant think nothing of curlers in the supermarket. I would support legislation to outlaw curlers, or men from supermarkets. I would prefer the curlers because ten minutes in a supermarket can drive a man to drink, and that's a great excuse.

On my way into the house the other day, I was reminded by a neighbor lady that I was the only man in the neighborhood that came home for lunch. At the time I dismissed the discussion as not being terribly significant. While I enjoy talking to the neighbors, the topic of coming home for lunch had just never crossed my mind. It did prompt some thought though, and some consideration as to why lunch at home was now becoming a way of life for me. First, I ruled out economics. You really don't save any money by eating at home. As a matter of fact, with my strange eating habits, it probably costs more. It wasn't ease. There are several restaurants as close to work as home. For that matter, distance has never been a deterrent to me if I wanted something enough. There is something special about home-cooked food, and my wife is certainly to be classified as an excellent cook, but as for lunches, even I can make soup, and the worst greasy spoon can't totally destroy a peanut butter sandwich. Finally, after much thought I came upon the answer. It's the hokey pokey. Now you have to go way back to remember the hokey pokey... that delightful dance where you put your elbow, heads, and other parts of your body in the circle, pull them out and proceed on. Personally, I never was anything akin to an Arthur Murray, but I do appreciate watching a good dance, and the hokey pokey done by a vivacious three-year-old to the refrains of a fifteen-year-old off-key singer and a poorly rehearsed bazooka band. Couple that with a report from the dancer on activities in the sand box, swings, and tree house. An update on the morning TV game shows, soap operas, and morning comics from her older sister, and all the entertainment for free. That's what takes me home for lunch. If Children's Records comes out with a 44-cent version of the bunny hop, you know I'll be the first in line to buy every copy in the city and distribute them to area restaurant jukeboxes. After all, it's just not fair for me to keep all these good times to myself.

I'm going to be taken to task for leaving my TV on all night and wasting energy, and I admit to being guilty of a crime just slightly less vicious than stealing squash from a neighbor'

s garden. Once in a while I do drop off to sleep during one of the more mediocre TV moments which could come anytime I am watching, but more likely late. Usually I wake up sometime in the middle of the night to an incessant shhhh and turn it off, but yesterday I slept through to the alarm clock and was upon waking pleased to rediscover Popeye on my television. I can't guess how many years it's been since I've seen Popeye, Olive Oil and Sweet Pea, so how could I possibly not lie there and watch the whole cartoon. As a youngster I did like Popeye, but regardless of how it transformed him, I just couldn't stomach spinach. Therefore, to rationalize my dislike for the vegetable I came to root for Bluto in every fight the two had, and of course that could number up to a dozen in a single cartoon… of course, Bluto never won the fight for Olive Oil. As I became a champion of the underdog, or more, the villain, I found myself liking the Coyote and despising the Road Runner. The Penguin, Riddler and Joker's exploits against the dynamic duo always found me cheering, and my childhood dreams were constantly filled with visions such as Tom devouring Jerry and Tweedy Bird being consumed in one gulp by Sylvester. It was only through the persistent efforts of others that I avoided a life of crime, and all because I didn't like spinach and rooted for the other guy. I doubt that my experiences related here will keep any parent from forcing unwanted vegetables on their children, but if you do notice unusual behavior, it could be as simple as too much summer squash. What we need is a superhero that functions best after he has consumed three ice cream sundaes. The problem there is carrying them. Inside his shirt it could drip down his leotards.

Flashbacks of memorable times of the past can be fun, but not at the expense of the present. For example, after days of diligent study, it came time for me to take the test to become a notary public. Off I went into the testing center. I arrived plenty early so there would be no rush, felt confident I knew the material, went into the room where the test was being administered, found a comfortable seat in an inconspicuous corner, and mentally prepared myself for the upcoming test. Someplace I once read or heard that a great number of tests are failed, not because of lack of knowledge, but because of tension and nervousness at test time, so I was fully prepared to keep myself cool and calm at all times, and I was until the lady with the tests walked into the room. She was slightly older with very curly, short gray hair, dark-rimmed glasses, a stern yet warm face, and what I call a matronly figure. She walked into the room out of "everybody's" classroom. Every man, woman, and child alive today has had a teacher that looked like this lady. With perfect posture, a determined walk, and the test cradled in her arm in such a way that no one would possibly dare grab one. She strode to the front of the room and my brow started to dampen. To the blackboard she went and with scratchy chalk wrote the name of the test and in big bold print, No Talking No Smoking, and my body started to perspire. Control I still had, until one smart lady sitting in front of me whispered in a voice just loud enough for me to hear. "It's just like taking a regent…" Flashbacks… cymbals, drums, twenty years earlier. Short hair, algebra, Latin, baseball, junior prom, driver training. The first date, social studies, drive-in movies, high school all over again… "And you're not to open the tests until I tell you to" and I was back to taking the test, just like before, with guts, a couple prayers and a lot of luck. Fortunately, I did remember my right name, it's ah…ah…ahh…or…

Have you ever noticed how people walk? There are so many different types of walks as there are people, and it's my theory that you can learn a great deal about a person by the way they walk. There have been studies on almost every kind of human behavior imaginable, and how different behaviors relate to personalities, so it wouldn't surprise me if there has been a walking study, but I've been doing a little study on my own. A couple of results so far: first, women are more difficult to study than men, because women seem to be more conscious of their walk and making sure it's ladylike. Probably every young girl has been subjected to a mother-daughter discussion of walking ladylike. Though as they get older, it appears that different lifestyles evidence themselves in walking. For example, a lady with a lot of children takes much smaller steps, conditioning from dodging in and out of toys and kids all over the floors. The other reason women are hard to research is because of the shoes they wear. The new styles with four-inch soles and six-inch heels obviously weigh somewhere in the neighborhood of fifteen pounds each from the way the wearers have to drag their feet to get around. For the men, there are a few distinct styles. First is the long step, usually found on a young man in his first executive job and impatient to move up. The bounce, too tired to take broad steps, but vigorous enough to keep on top. This step is also a favorite of short people who use it in crowds to see over the top of other people's heads. There's the toe dragger, usually found to be used by obstinate characters fighting every move anyone, including themselves makes. Then there's the graceful charger. His steps are somewhat like those of a beginning ballet dancer. It's made up of a small leap, a little slide on the ball of the foot and bringing up the following foot to land perpendicular to the forward heel. This person is usually floundering in his life and is satisfied easily by such things as getting from here to there without falling down. There's one other style… it's a hop on one foot, perfected by people like myself who still have to get around, even though we've usually got one foot in the mouth.

I happened by an old-fashioned farmers' market the other day, where the various vendors had their wares, or in this case, produce spread out on makeshift tables, backs of trucks, the ground, and even the hoods of cars. Everything from fresh picked pickled peaches to freshly gathered eggs could be bought direct from the man or woman that does the growing. I saw a table of home-baked bread and pastries, wrapped in cellophane to display appealingly the look that only home-baked products can give, and all of this on sale to surprisingly few people led me to wonder about shoppers. Now, it's perhaps possible that people just didn't know about this particular farmers' market, and of course there could be dozens of other reasons why it wasn't doing well, but it's possible that even for saving and freshness, people won't go out of their way. Normally I am one of that type. It's much easier for me to do the most expedient. If I'm after food, a supermarket where I can get everything I want in one stop is generally the route I take, rather than shopping for individual items. Of course, there are the shoppers that will spend a dollars' worth of gas to save fifteen cents on a can of green beans, but for them, I suspect shopping is more of an avocation than a necessity. I don't know if there's dickering going on for prices, but that would make the farmers market even more fun. Imagine having a good healthy argument with the lettuce salesman about whether you are going to pay 25-cents a head or get two for .45. There are all kinds of possibilities. People could take out all their hostilities in a very harmless way by arguing over the price of a nice eggplant. With the growth of flea markets where you can buy out somebody else's attic, the direct person-to-person sales have advantages. It shouldn't, and I wouldn't want it to hurt regular retail businesses, but then, how can I tell a specially marked can of peas that I only want to pay 19-cents? Did you ever argue with a computer… and win?

I remember last winter talking to a grandmother who was telling me about her grandchildren who wanted to go ice skating at the new skating rink, but decided against it because they couldn't find anyone to give them a ride and didn't feel like walking. I remember as a youngster being told by my father about his walks to and from school. Of course, each time he told the story, it grew more and more difficult for him to trudge through the shoulder-high snow, ankle-deep mud and broiling sun, and the mileage he walked was never the same. Sometimes it was only a mile, a couple of times I think he told the story with up to five miles between his house and school, but each story was designed to dramatically illustrate how soft the youngsters of my generation had it. Well, yesterday I drove by a couple different schools on a short trip I had to make, and it impressed me that maybe it is time that we gave our kids the basis for a story like my fathers they can use later on. What impressed this on me was one school in particular where there must have been sixty school busses if there was one. When I tell you that the school parking lot was a literal sea of yellow bus-tops, I'm not even exaggerating, and I just couldn't imagine how one school system, even granted that it is a large one, could use that many busses. The more I drove, the more I thought about it, and wondered if it might not be a good idea to start reassessing school transportation. There are those that have to ride busses to school. They do live far for walking, but with the energy situation and higher and higher prices of fuel, maybe the school systems should drop back a bit. In some areas, I know there are no sidewalks, and kids would have to walk on busy roads, but the school districts should push on the municipalities involved to get sidewalks laid. A sidewalk will last longer than a gallon of gas... Anyways, when I was a kid we lived two blocks from the school and riding the bus wasn't a problem. Everyone can't live two blocks away from school, but everyone can learn to walk a little more.

One phenomenon of the modern day is the garage sale. I can think of the time when only people that the rest of society looked down on would pick through other people's garbage, yet nowadays you can hardly drive down a street in any town and not see at least one sign advertising a garage sale. Some of the real estate companies have garage sale signs they'll loan free for one or two days to people that are going into the retail business. Some newspapers have free kits on how to run a successful garage sale that they give out when people place their classified ads, and aside from the people that just want to clean out their attics, there are groups that will sponsor garage sales as fundraisers. Some of the reasons for garage sales include the ever-increasing mobility of our society. Most of us have relatives that were born in a particular house, have lived all their lives there, and will probably pass away there, but anymore, those are the minority. Most people move once, twice, three or four times during their lifetimes. Many a lot more, and when you're moving you can't truck around the toys that kids have outgrown, paperback books that have been read and reread, clothes that have been outgrown, and the hundreds of other things that one can find at a garage sale. Of course, the other part of garage sale motivation is the different way we buy things. Your grandmother probably bought a couch, figuring it was going to last for thirty or forty years. Now it seems that we change our furniture like we change our socks. Decorating schemes may not match, size may not be just right for the new room arrangement, or for whatever the reason, we don't expect the same length of service from the merchandise we buy, so out it goes on the lawn, in the garage, on the porch, or wherever we can find a few square feet of unused space that can be converted to a selling area for a couple of days. There are people who have made it almost an occupation to go from garage sale to sale on weekends looking for bargains, and it is certainly a measure of success that the state was considering making those that had garage sales collect sales tax. This weekend millions of people can drift from house to house searching for bargains and measuring how others live. Buy what they're selling at the uniquely American garage sale.

That time of year... for a good many people it's already started. For more, this coming weekend will mark the start, and there will be some that will try to wait another week or so, but it's inevitable that for everyone with a school age child, before the first week of September gets here, it will be back-to-school shopping time. Usually when you mention back-to school-shopping, clothes come to mind. There are shoes, sneakers, dresses, slacks, shirts, sweaters, socks, and the rest. It's absolutely amazing how much the kids have grown since this procedure was last gone through, and even when last year's socks couldn't fit, it's enough to make a parent tear out any hair they might have left. Aside from the clothes, there are dozens of other items to collect, from pencils and notebooks to things to carry them in, and I happened through a store the other day and saw a young family torturing themselves over the selection of another apparent must for many back-to-schoolers. The lunch pail. Well, I never really thought about it and I have to admit to having personally avoided that part of back to school shopping in our family, but the more I watched and listened to this family talking about lunch boxes, the more I saw that it could indeed be the most difficult part of all selections that have to be made in the next three weeks. I think most of the kids that brought lunch when I was in school had two choices: they either had those old-fashioned black lunch pails with the thermos that fits in the top, or there was the brown paper sack. That sack was convenient because it only required a one-way trip and could be thrown away after one use or be folded conveniently for carrying the rest of the day in a back pocket. But now there are dozens of ways to choose from, depending on who is the most popular young star at the time for most sales. There are, of course, the cartoon pails that are also popular, like the old standards of Mickey Mouse and Donald Duck, but new things like Star Wars characters are popular, and for little girls, the Holly Hobbie lunch pails are popular. There is plastic and metal, depending on your preference and they carry a sandwich that will probably get traded to a kid who has to buy his lunch at school.

One of the characteristics of our society is that we sometimes move too fast. That's not to say that it's always wrong to be in high gear and full speed ahead, but sometimes I think we get going so fast that we miss some of the pleasures that come with taking life a little easier. It used to be that business and general living conditions were fast just in the cities... the big cities. How many times have you heard people, after a visit to New York City, for example, come back and say something to the effect that they just couldn't live there because everything is too fast for them? Well, I've got news for you. In case you haven't paid attention lately, there are very few people now that visit a large city and come back with that attitude. Some of it is because the pace isn't all that different at home and the city residents haven't slowed down. Some of the change comes because there is a narrowing gap between city and non-city living. Some has to do with suburbs spreading out further and further. Some is transportation, meaning it's easier to get back and forth between, and thus a trip to the city is a common occurrence now, rather than a once-a-year event. The reason I started thinking about this is because a week or so ago, I had to travel about halfway across the state and back, and when I make these ventures, it's generally on the thruway, where traffic moves at least five to ten miles per hour over the speed limit, and sightseeing is limited to reading the sides of trailer trucks and counting campers you pass. So, it was this one day I felt like slowing down just a little bit and take my drive back on the side roads, most of them well-traveled, some feed routes to small cities that serve as commerce centers for a particular area, but also through some pretty little villages where people sit on the front porch to read the Sunday paper, squirrels play tag high above the tree-lined streets, and where Sunday drivers go at least five to ten miles under the speed limit. Admittedly, this was a Sunday afternoon, and the hustle and bustle of these little villages would be upped on Monday, but in some of these places, there seems to be a kind of absorption of the pace. It took me about an hour longer to get home, but I was far more ready for the Monday morning pace.

Up until I was six or seven years old, we lived with one set of my grandparents. That was back during the war when my father was overseas and my mother, brother and I lived at her parents' house. Those were nice days for me, and my grandfather was an excellent surrogate father during those formative years when my own father was away. Even though he passed away many, many years ago, I can still picture him as clear as day, and no grandson who was the little angel could forget the man whose one purpose during those young years of mine was to keep me happy. My grandmother on my mother's side was equally good to me, and no one ever has, or ever will bake a chocolate cake exactly like hers. My father's parents were also good grandparents, and as a matter of fact, as I sit here thinking back to those early years, I can't help but reflect on how lucky I really was that I had such grandmas and grandpas. I guess I'll always remember that one day my grandfather and grandmother Rich came to our house to visit. We had been expecting them and my brother and I always looked forward to their visits, but never in a thousand years would I have guessed that on this one particular visit they would bring with them two brand new bicycles, a blue one and a red one. Undoubtedly there are lots of people that don't have as fond memories of their grandparents as I do, but our kids I know will have fond memories of their grandparents when they get to be my age.

Visits with Grandma Rich were always a treat, and a phone call from Grandma and Grandpa Brown all the way from San Francisco always made me happy, so maybe it's a good idea. The congress has approved a measure that would make Grandparents Day the first Sunday after Labor Day every year. Just like on Father's Day or Mother's Day, sometimes we tend to overdo with the gifts and the hoopla that goes with it, but it may not be that bad an idea to take one day out of the year to pay special attention to grandparents, because they are special people and deserve a little special recognition. Sometimes I tend to be just a bit cynical about things like this and jump on it as nothing more than a florist promotion or the like, but where else can you go for ice cream every night, get to stay up way past bedtime, not eat your spinach, and hear previously untold stories of your childhood escapades? It all happens at Grandma's and Grandpa's, and it's worth a special day.

For centuries there have been poets that have written about the changing of colors from the summer greens to the fall mixtures, so I'm sure you're familiar with it. Even if you've never in your life read a piece of poetry about it, I would find it hard to believe that you haven't experienced in some way one of those beautiful days of early fall. This weekend we were graced with a couple of those days, and I found myself in the middle of spectacular surroundings. I ended up riding a bus around the southern tier of the state, around Oneonta and Binghamton, which is another story I will probably share with you sometime. In that area it is very hilly and as you rode to the crest of one hill and looked over a valley, there was just no way that you couldn't be impressed. There were still some very deep greens, yet they blended in so nicely with the yellows, golds, oranges, browns, rusts, and seemingly dozens of other shades in between. Somehow the pleasure of the early fall days is made even more delightful because we know that not far behind comes the bareness of the branches and the cold winter winds blowing through the same openings where the autumn sun dances in and out with its golden rays. We could just keep going on. Truly these days give Mother Nature the opportunity to perform at her best, and it's a show that everyone should take advantage of. If next week, Saturday or Sunday, the weather is nice, jump in your car, forget the price of gas for one day, and take a drive. Get off the regular path, out into the country, off into the woods, and see for yourself. Make mental pictures and keep them secure. Then, a couple of months from now, when the snow is piled high, the winter winds howl, and you're bundled up keeping warm, you'll at least have the memory of beauty to go with the beast.

Last year, the city cut down the two trees in the front of my house, which was a happy day in our lives. We were happy because the trees got cut down before a good windstorm knocked them down, and because it was going to eliminate a considerable amount of fall leaf-raking. That's not to say the front is completely void of leaves, because I don't think there is a square foot of land anywhere in the country that avoids falling leaves, and because leaf raking isn't one of my favorite pastimes. I wasn't looking forward to seeing the day I had to go out there. There are some people I have noticed driving around that will rake their leaves almost daily, only to have to face each day more and more of what Mother Nature obliges by keeping the leaves coming as fast as they can be picked up. Me, I wait until they are all down, and if snow hasn't arrived, then I'll rake. Well, anyway, there were leaves on my front yard when I left for work yesterday morning and there were leaves again this morning, but when I got home from work yesterday the fallen leaves were gone... but so were the neighbor's, and the house on the other side of them, and up and down the street... all the fallen leaves were gone. Well, not completely gone. They'd all been transported down the street a few houses to one of the larger leaf piles I've seen in some time. It seems the kids in the neighborhood weren't content with the amount of leaves they could find in any one yard, so they went around collecting all the neighborhood leaves to use for their fun. What they had built was a leaf fort- or fortune- as our three-year-old called it, with walls that were about three feet high and a well-packed center to provide an excellent landing pad for jumping from an adjacent small incline. The leaves had been hauled in wagons, doll carriages and anything else they could find to carry them in, and the whole experience was nice for the neighborhood. The kids loved it and no one minded having their leaves carried away--even the lady whose yard became a giant leaf pile didn't seem to mind, and I told the kids they could play that game right through the winter. Snow piles are fun, and I know I can contribute more.

One world...and we'll talk about that...

Back in the days when I was in high school it was almost imperative that you take a foreign language if you wanted to go to college. At that time, a good many colleges required that you have a minimum of two years language study...and they didn't specify what language...so I took Latin. Don't ask me why...because even though I'm old, I'm not old enough to have been around when Latin was a language used to communicate between countries. Aside from amo, amas, amat and et tu brute, I don't remember anything...As a matter of fact, I don't think I did any day after I got out of class. I've been involved in projects from time to time that in retrospect could be called a waste of time. Certainly taking Latin would rank near the top...and now aside from a few slang words in three or four languages, it's impossible for me to communicate with someone who speaks in a different language. It's no solace, but the odds are that you're in the same category as I. According to a study that has just come out, Americans' lack of ability to communicate in foreign languages threatens the economy and national security. The study done by a presidential commission suggests that, among other things, colleges and schools be given up to forty dollars per year per student studying a foreign language and that a foreign language again become a requirement for college admission. Only 8-percent require it now...and that's down from thirty-four percent, twelve years ago. There are a lot of other parts of the study that would seem to make sense if you consider, for example, that the Japanese have ten thousand English-speaking business representatives in the United States; we have 900 over there, and only a few speak Japanese. It would seem to put us at a disadvantage in competing in the international market...

and as the world comes closer and closer to being one big shopping center, it's even more important...and if you hear of any country that's considering changing their national language back to Latin let me know.

The answer went with him...and we'll talk about that...

I don't remember the first time I saw a circus...but I'll never forget the first time I saw Ringling Brothers' Barnum and Bailey circus. They were, many years ago...and still are, for that matter, the Tiffany of the circus world. Back when I saw Ringling Brothers for the first time, they were still in a tent...and I remember the spectacle that went with their performance...the girls in their spangled costumes...the animals...the daring young man on the flying trapeze...and the clowns. That was the first time that I saw weary Willie...sweeping up the spotlight...I don't remember if he did that or not...but later on that was to become the trademark of that particular clown...but I remember that there was something about the act that made Emmett Kelley stand out from all the other clowns...and they had some great ones at Ringling Brothers' Barnum and Bailey circuses. Anyway, this week, weary Willie...Emmett Kelley...passed away at the age of eighty...after having spent fifty-eight years of transforming himself daily from a man that looked like any other person... could have been a doctor...a store clerk...a truck driver...into a world of fantasy where no one looks the way they really do... where everything is bigger than life...and where the rewards come in the form of laughs from an appreciative audience.

By now you've probably already heard several times about the life of Emmett Kelley...starting out as a cartoonist...drawing weary Willie...bringing him to life over his own body...traveling with Ringling Brothers until a labor dispute ended their relationship about twenty years ago...and then out on his own to perform for millions and become even more the world's most famous clown. It's hard to understand why people found weary Willie funny. Aside from the antics, weary Willie was a sad character. His mouth drooped...his eyes looked forlorn...his clothes were tattered., .and even with the most famous part of his act, the spotlight sweeping, his character was frustrated...yet we laughed...and laughed...some I suspect because being bigger than life, the clown character had just a little bit of all of us in him...and we could laugh at ourselves and never know it...but more...it was the ability of Emmett Kelley to make us laugh... and with his passing we lost a little bit of that *something we all need more of. Sometimes even a little smile can help.*

Just a country boy...and we'll talk about that...

Maybe it was just me and those things that were of value to me growing up...maybe it's the times they are a changin'...or maybe it's a combination of both...but it seems to me that the junior prom and the senior ball never were all that important. Of course, I was a guy and I guess that has something to do with it...because now my contact with the high school age is primarily through the eyes of a sixteen-year-old girl...but I don't remember it being all that big a deal for me. It was more than just another school dance...but one of the differences...the big differences is the attire. Back when I was a teenager there was one kind of tuxedo. It was black...and when you rented it you got all the accessories...the shirt, plain white... The studs...the cuff links, the cummerbund...and that was that. If you were really well off, you already had black shoes...if you had a little extra money and no black shoes, you went and bought some...and if you were investing all your money in the tux and the flowers, you wore your brown shoes and hoped the gym would be dark.

Nowadays, I understand the girls have to make their dress selections early so that the guys will know what color tuxedo to get so as not to clash with the dress. If anyone in our school had come to a dance with a pastel tuxedo he would have gotten run out of town within five minutes. Of course, there was an alternative. That was the white dinner jacket. You could rent one of those... still get all the accessories and feel formal. Brown shoes went better with the white coat. Anyway...by the time the junior prom rolled around, most had their driver's license...the problem was getting the car... And Jimmy Carter didn't work any harder on Begin and Sadat than I had to on my father just to let me have one night. Youngsters I think almost always win in those particular situations…parents, I guess just have that one little memory…maybe of their big nights…and making prom night special is a tradition that is passed down from generation to generation through pleadings for the automobile. I was reminded of all this the other day when I found myself suddenly in the older generation…and I realized how things have changed….I never even took my date to dinner before the dance…who could afford to take the chance of spilling spaghetti sauce on brown shoes.

Too bad...and we'll talk about that...

We've been advertising on this radio station for the past several weeks the different fairs that are occurring in the area, and there was the story in this morning's paper about how the poor Seneca County fair has run into some bad luck with the weather for the first two days of their fair this year...and it got me to thinking about county fairs and my experiences with them. I haven't been a regular at any fair for a few years, but I remember as a youth, there wasn't a year went by that we didn't go to several of them. One of the fairs was near our home, and that's the one that really sticks in my mind.

When the fair week arrived, it was in a sense, one of the big social events of the season. There were people who maybe only saw each other a couple of times a year, but you could be sure one of those occasions would be at the fair. It was something to get a ribbon for a vegetable that was particularly big...or a flower display that was especially attractive...and for a farmer that won a prize for a pig or cow...chicken or sheep, the fair provided incentive to show even better stock the next year.

Of course, to a youngster, the fair was the midway. That was when the rest of the world came to our little town. The barkers... The sideshow people...the roustabouts...the people that never seemed to live in a town like ours were there for us to see...as much an attraction as the rides and games they manned. Very few youngsters didn't go home without a stomach ache from too much cotton candy, candy apples, salt water taffy, and hot dogs...and of course every young man fantasized about the one side show with the strippers, where they stripped to more than you see girls on the beach wearing today...as a matter of fact, it's not limited to the beach…but that was the fair. That was grown men taking an afternoon off from work to watch horse racing without a single pari-mutuel window…and it was free rulers, yard sticks and enough literature to last for a year from the merchants' displays. It was big time stars performing on the grandstand. Stars you'd never heard of…before…or after…and it was waiting for the whole thing to start up again the next year…and I never remember a rainy day. Maybe my memory is failing me.

I didn't know him that well…after all, when I was growing up… and in the area where I grew up, other people's fathers weren't around that much when work was a six day week…and that left little time for just being around for other kids to see. I couldn't write a eulogy for the man because I don't think I even knew where he worked…but he was the father of a friend of mine and that counted for something. The other day I was reading a newspaper from a neighboring city and I came across the obituary of a man whose son had been one of my childhood friends. Because I didn't know the man, there was little for me to remember about him, but as often happens in situations where something triggers the back of the mind, I could see the man's house just as plainly as if it were only yesterday. It was on a corner and at the top of a small hill. They had a nice yard where softball games were often played. They had a basketball net and backboard nailed up on their garage where many hours were spent…and because their house was kind of in the middle of several friends' homes, it was a natural place for gathering. My house was on the same street as the school so it was a good spot to stop for warming… and there certainly lots of hours played there…but often it was my friend's house where we all ended up.

It's funny because I have absolutely no idea where any of those friends are anymore. For one reason or another I've never kept in touch with any of them…and while their names come back to me if I think about it…and I can remember what they looked like twenty or so years ago, I wonder how many I would recognize if I saw them today…or how many world recognize me. I only mention all this because I saw that obituary and just for a moment it sent me back to that little village of my youth…

and the people that lived there. Life wasn't all that simple in those days...it wasn't any easier I suspect that it is today. It was easier for me but only because life tends to complicate itself as we grow older... And I sipped my coffee and read the small story on the man's death...saw an imaginary jump shot in his driveway basketball court and continued on...but I couldn't let it pass completely without sharing that little moment...because the man was survived by great grandchildren...which made that imaginary basket a lot harder to hit.

A reminder…and we'll talk about that…

It may be that I don't spend enough time in the kitchen to realize that some things aren't as old fashioned as I thought they were…or it may be that the time I was there, we just happened on one old fashioned can…or the product we bought was extremely old. Well, I think I can reasonably rule out the third possibility…so that leaves the first two…and I suspect that we just came across a company that still puts out its product in an old style can. The style I'm talking about is the kind with the little key that's attached to the bottom…which you remove and then use to wind up a band of metal around the edge for opening.

I hadn't seen one of those in years and then last night I happened to be in the kitchen while my wife was fixing dinner and she gave me a can to open. I started toward the electric can opener… after all…our kitchen has all the modern conveniences…and then discovered the little key. I was like a kid again, because that used to be one of my favorite jobs. It was a challenge for young fingers to avoid getting cut while working around the can…it was a challenge to get all around the can without having the metal slip off the key and then be faced with the even larger challenge of figuring out how to open the can the rest of the way…and sometimes, the key would even snap off before you got all the way around. I guess I'd forgotten the shush of air that came rushing out with the first twist of the key on a coffee can…I'd forgotten how to hold the can in one hand, the key in another, and turn one at the same time you tried not to drop the other. There were a lot of challenges that went with the key opening cans…and it's funny that something so small could hold poignancy. I'm happy to report that my manual dexterity has improved from the early days as a kitchen helper and I got all the way around the can…and quite fast, I might add…without a major accident of any kind. There were no cut fingers…the method worked to perfection…and my wife went on with the preparation of dinner… As for me…I decided I'd go shopping with her just to look for more cans with key opening tops. I'd forgotten how much fun it could be to help.

We watched til dawn together so many times.
Oh, so many times.
We watched the sunset together so many times.
Oh, so many times.
Together we shared so many laughs.
Oh, so many laughs.
We cried so many times.
And we walked side by side.
We shared,
And we loved.
Oh, so much love and so much time
Oh, that it will never end…
Thank you for the dawns, the sunsets and the love.
And most of all thank you for the time.

CPSIA information can be obtained
at www.ICGtesting.com
Printed in the USA
LVHW030437021220
673097LV00007B/257

9 781977 229342